Pancho threw back his head and  laugh.

Then the table hit him . . . Right behind the table came Sloane. He followed in a high leap, one foot descending to push Pancho's teeth down his throat, the other kicking the gun from his hand . . .

'You wanted boots,' Sloane reminded him, closing in, 'try these for size.'

Pancho's hand was an inch short of his pistol when Sloane's boot stamped down on it. Sloane ground the hand into the floor like it was an old cigar butt. Screaming an oath, Pancho tore free his hand. Sloane kicked the gun aside . . . and slammed him against the table . . . Pancho flopped onto the floor . . .

The remaining five friends of Pancho Gonzalez still sitting at their table had been as stunned as everyone else . . . Now they sprang up, sharpened metal glittering in their hands . . .

Also by Steve Lee in the *Sloane* series

SLOANE: THE FASTEST FIST IN THE WEST

Steve Lee

Sloane:
Fistful of Hate

Futura Publications Limited

A Futura Book

First published in Great Britain in 1974
by Futura Publications Limited
Reprinted 1975

ISBN 0 8600 71006

Printed in Great Britain by
Hazell Watson & Viney Ltd
Aylesbury, Bucks

Futura Publications Limited
49 Poland Street,
London, W1A 2LG

PROLOGUE

Rearing up from a sterile expanse of barren red earth like heaven-pointed fingers, the square white towers of the mission of San Pietro suggested a fortress rather than a place of worship. And like a fortress it had squatted on the red dust for over two hundred years, stubbornly resisting the attacks of man and nature, of Indians, bandits, droughts and hurricanes. It would stand forever an old priest had foretold many years before, a tribute to the faith of the humble people of Lascara.

Such devout faith demanded to be put to the test thought Don Luis Fernando de Silviera y Castilia as, from the cover of a verdant patch of low-lying manzanita, he trained his binoculars on the whitewashed adobe of the mission, his long uncalloused fingers teasing the instrument into focus.

It was Sunday and a slack procession of penitents tramped the rutted path from the village of Lascara to the mission, the favoured amongst them carrying colourful banners of the saints which hung limply from their staffs in the hot, windless air. They were mostly *peons* and their families. Against the bleakness of the arid landscape, the men looked crisp and bright in their best white cotton pants and shirts. The fortunate ones led burros on the backs of which small children swayed. The women, all but the youngest in black, walked in the footsteps of their sons and husbands, their heads piously lowered. To Don Luis they had the appearance of a flock of starving crows pacing the soil, beaks dipped in the hope of a tasty worm. Shifting the binoculars he spied a taller, black-robed figure waiting beside the open doors of the mission. One of those treacherous dogs of a priest he realised and his proud Spanish features contracted in anger.

From behind came a hissing whisper: 'Is it not as I have told, my chief? A nest of traitors, of guerrilleros . . .'

Ramon, *mozo* to Don Luis, wriggled on his elbows through the brush to join his master.

'With my own eyes I have seen those pigs of priests carry three wounded rebels inside, to care for them as a mother cares for her children!'

Don Luis gravely lowered the binoculars.

'If it is as you have said, Ramon, you will be well rewarded.'

'*Muchas gracias*, my chief,' said Ramon, dipping his head in thanks, his dark face beaming.

'And the widows of Lascara, every one of them, will have to say a mass for the souls of their dead sons,' Don Luis promised.

Together the two men shrank back through the brush and scrambled down the slight knoll behind which their horses and thirty armed men awaited them.

If anyone had been unfortunate enough suddenly to make the acquaintance of these men, each of them mounted on a fine horse, they would have seen a tough gang of leather-faced *vaqueros* such as might be found on any large ranch – except perhaps that they were still more arrogant and cruel in their expressions than is usual even amongst that hardened breed of men. But to Don Luis Fernando de Silviera they were a troop of cavalry of the National Army of the Liberation. He was their commander, and he was about to give them the order to attack.

At the first sound of the galloping horsemen, the villagers turned with lazy unhurried interest to watch their approach, not even pausing on their solemn trek towards the mission. Since Lascara lay on the route that wound inland from the border at Mexicali, cutting deeper into the interior of Baja California, such large parties of riders were not unfamiliar. Seldom did they stop however, finding the village too sleepy for their fast ways – for which deliverance the pious folk of Lascara weekly raised their voices to God in thanks.

So the villagers continued their sober barefoot progress towards the mission and waited to taste the dust of those men of polished leather and steel who would thunder past, anxious to the point of madness to reach a distant place that would undoubtedly disappoint them when they reached it. The villagers had no such fine horses nor leather boots with jangling spurs yet they could afford to feel superior for, surely, in faith and piety there were none richer in all the world than the hard-working men and women of Lascara.

But these furiously galloping horsemen were like none that had ever passed through the village before. Their business was not elsewhere but at this very place. They rode straight at the procession, their voices merging in a rising cheer of excitement. When they did not slow their break-neck pace, unease spread amongst the villagers ... unease that rapidly became fear when they saw the faces of the *vaqueros*, fear that burst into fragmenting panic when the first shots exploded. Suddenly crying children echoed their mothers' screams. The charging *vaqueros* smashed through the column of penitents as a fierce wave sweeps away a sand-castle. The column disintegrated. Those that still lived ran for the sanctuary of the mission.

Don Luis and his cavalry fanned out, hacking at the frantically running figures with shards of polished sunlight. Those that fell beneath their blades lay writhing, the red soil becoming redder beneath them. Yelling their triumph, the horsemen whirled their dripping sabres above their heads, wheeling in pursuit of further game ...

The doors of the mission were not wide. Wedged against them, a tight-packed mass of humanity pleaded for admit-

7

tance. Children, women and men struggled to push through to safety. Those already safe inside struggled with equal desperation to shut the wooden doors on fast-approaching death.

Above, in one of the towers, a weeping man attacked the mission's great bell with a metal bar, beating out a belated alarm that boomed insistently across the sunburnt plain. As if in reply a rain of bullets hammered the bell, tolling an angry, stammering tune. The man with the metal bar stumbled, his white clothes suddenly pocked with red splashes, and fell against the swaying bell. It met him with a dull indignant roar, tossing him from the tower to break in the dust eighty feet below.

Before a shroud of dust had settled over the body, Don Luis rode up to the mission, his men a firm wall at his back. Into the shrieking crowd laying siege to the mission doors they emptied their pistols. Death reaped a good plentiful harvest. Bodies collected against the doors, whole families heaped together in a final embrace. Slugs ripped through living flesh, raked the dead wood behind.

The doors swung together, those inside trying with mad urgency to shut them against the attackers. The villagers trapped between the closing doors and the guns of the *vaqueros* cried out in despair, begging to be admitted. A youth thrust his hands through the narrowing gap between the doors and tried to force his way inside. The doors closed on his hands, snapping the bones of his fingers, grinding them to fragments. His screams shrilled through the roar of gunfire. He tore his hands free and held the ribboned fingers before his eyes. A bullet slapped the horror off his face, flung him onto a twitching heap of his comrades.

Shut out from the mission, the remaining villagers turned and stumbled wide-armed towards their murderers, pleading mercy from God and the *vaqueros*. Through a curtain of harsh smoke, Don Luis and his men watched them advance.

8

They reacted to pleas for mercy as if they were well-told jokes. Into the ranks of wailing villagers they laughingly poured a fusillade. The bullets punched them this way and that, spinning them round in a macabre dance that ended face-down in the bloodied dust.

Presently there were only killers and killed outside the walls of the mission of San Pietro. Those who could not afford horses or boots had no money for guns and there were few firing pieces inside the mission; but these few were soon heard to speak. More than one of Don Luis' army sagged in the saddle or fell, blasted from his horse.

The *vaqueros* dismounted behind the mission, out of the line of fire of the defenders. Backs against the walls, hidden from the overlooking windows, they worked their way back to the mission doors and regrouped.

The priests had placed a bench against one wall of the mission so that the old ones might sit shaded and take their ease. Don Luis' voice rose in command. In a moment four of his men were battering the doors with the bench. At the third charge, a musket belched smoke from a window. One of the men carrying the bench cried out and pitched forward to join the bodies of those he had helped kill. Another man ran to take his place.

Covered by a steady fire directed at the windows, the four men continued to pound the doors with the battering-ram. At each impact the ancient doors shook and the wooden bar holding the doors shut was heard to groan under the strain. A few more attempts and the *vaqueros* were rewarded by the cracking whine of snapping wood. The doors burst inwards. Don Luis led his men, cheering and laughing, through the gap, shoving aside a flimsy barricade of chairs and benches. They found themselves in church. Facing them stood a single man, a priest with an old Spanish musket raised to his shoulder. The sudden stillness was destroyed by the roar of the musket. Its load smacked against the wall high above Don Luis' head. About him, some of the *vaqueros* raised a mocking laugh, as much from relief as amusement.

The priest let the musket drop. His face was disturbingly calm. He made no move to escape when Ramon stepped towards him.

'*Cabron!*' the *mozo* hissed from between yellowed teeth and with slow deliberation he cut the priest's throat, releasing a fast gush of blood that splashed hotly on the bare stone floor of the church.

Ramon yelled back to his companions: 'Remember, *muchachos*, kill only the *ugly* women!' Roaring their delight the *vaqueros* raised their rifles and sabres high in the air and pushed forward after Don Luis, trampling the body of the priest.

They swept through the church, overturning plaster effigies of Christ, of headless bleeding saints, and of the Holy Mother weeping tears of blood.

Most of the villagers had taken refuge in the mission patio. To one side of the open courtyard, by the small vineyard, a bed of white roses had been carefully nurtured. Amongst the pale blooms a young woman and her baby lay together, their eyes closed as if in sleep. It was a sleep from which neither of them would ever awaken. The knife which had taken their lives was still limply clutched in the hand of the mother who had preferred to embrace Death rather than a cruel-faced *vaquero*.

The remaining women cowered in a corner of the patio, some whispering words of comfort to bawling children. Between them and the *vaqueros* the last of the menfolk stood in a defiant line. Each man held the weapon with which he had chosen to die: a knife from the kitchen, an axe, a rake ... They launched themselves at the *vaqueros* streaming into the courtyard, striking out with the desperation of men without futures, men who are already dead and wish

10

to see many of their enemies die with them. At least three of Don Luis' army fell beneath their hacking frenzy, two bleeding to death, a third blinded for life ... It was over quicker than it takes a man to plant his seed inside a woman. A scattered burst of firing, a slashing flurry of sabres and the men of Lascara were no more.

The *vaqueros* fell upon the women as starving dogs fall upon scraps of meat. Don Luis watched them coldly, his delicate lips pressed tight together. At times his men disgusted him. Yet he made no move to interfere. He knew that if animals are to remain loyal, they have to be fed.

He walked stiffly over to where Ramon, assisted by three others, was helping an unwilling young girl, a child, out of her clothes. The dress at which they were tearing was white, for that day was to have been the day of her first Communion. Rusty stains streaked the dress – the blood of her brother.

'Ramon ...'

'Si, *Jefecito* ...' Ramon grinned. 'You wish perhaps to be first with this beauty who, I am sure, no man has touched but her father?'

Don Luis glanced at the thin underfed body revealed beneath the tattered dress, looked into the wild, terrified eyes of the girl. He shook his head.

'Where are they, these rebels?' he asked his *mozo*. Ramon motioned towards one of the square towers of the mission, the one that was not a bell-tower.

'Come,' said Don Luis, turning on his heel, stepping over corpses as he crossed the courtyard towards the low wooden door at the foot of the tower.

Following him, Ramon looked back over his shoulder with regret at the struggling girl pinned beneath one of his companions, her wide-spread legs kicking up the dust. He shrugged. The *chica* could wait. Others would smooth his way.

11

Don Luis waited for Ramon to open the door. Ramon struggled with the latch without success. The door was bolted from inside.

'Like the girl, the door must be broken before she can be entered,' Ramon chuckled.

Raising his pistol, Don Luis blasted the door. It swung open before Ramon's touch. The two men entered the tower. Pistols in hand, they climbed the coiling stairs, their spurs clattering loudly against the stone steps.

As they neared the top, they advanced more cautiously. If there were rebels in the tower they would be armed and waiting. Another turn of the corkscrew stairs and they might be looking into the barrels of their pistols ... Ramon hesitated. He looked back for instructions. Don Luis nodded for him to proceed. With little enthusiasm, Ramon edged round the corner.

Two shots rang out almost immediately, sounding strangely loud and resonant inside the tower of stone. Ramon tumbled back past Don Luis and lay sprawled head-down across the stairs, hands clutched to the ugly red flower blossoming from his belly.

Don Luis inched forward and loosed off a shot at a figure glimpsed in a dark doorway above, jerking back instantly as an answering shot powdered stone close to his cheek. Don Luis reloaded with his back to the wall. He thought bitterly of his useless *vaqueros* chasing pleasure down below whilst he alone faced a dangerous band of cornered rebels. What if they should realise that he was but one man, a general without his army? Don Luis' hands trembled as he slotted cartridges. Nearby, Ramon moaned loudly and unpleasantly.

Don Luis began to retreat down the stairs, a step at a time. He would return with more men. It was not cowardice, he told himself, but strategy ... Abruptly two more shots echoed down from above. They did not seem to have been aimed at him. Don Luis listened ... The ravished women wailed. There was no other sound, for Ramon's moans had ended and with them his life. There had been a finality about those last shots, thought Don Luis. Suddenly his fear was gone. He knew he had to see what waited above. He advanced impulsively up the stairs, taking cover where he found it.

No blaze of guns greeted him at the top of the stairs. Only a calm silence, completely empty of life. Edging forward behind his pistol, Don Luis peered into the dark room before him. Close by the door, in murky half-light, three men lay awkwardly positioned by death. Three ... Ramon had said there were three. One of them looked as if he had been dead for hours. The other bodies still bled. Don Luis realised that the trapped rebels had killed themselves rather than endure the tortures they would undoubtedly have suffered at the hands of the *vaqueros*.

He followed his pistol into the room. There were no windows and it took several seconds for his eyes to adjust to the dark. Sombre drapes, dark as old wine, curtained the room. Against them hung paintings depicting tortured saints and scenes from the crucifixion, painful in their detail. At the far end of the room rose a black-veiled altar flickeringly illuminated by candles and dozens of tapers, slim and white, like the fingers of ghostly hands raised in prayer. From the altar a pair of dead, empty eyes contemplated Don Luis. Don Luis' breath tightened in his throat. His heart hammered. He crossed himself, the first time in years.

Back at his hacienda, Don Luis had many objects of beauty but none equalled the beauty of that which stared at him from the altar. It was a human skull – yet no skull that had ever been clothed by the flesh of man. Its beauty was ethereal, delicate as a snowflake. It was both ice and fire, frost and flame. Beneath the glacial features, behind the death-mask smile, red threads of vein seemed to pulse, dancing with life. The hollow eyes burned in darkness, blazing

13

like sun-fired rubies. To look into the depths of those eyes was to see the molten pits of Hell.

The moment Don Luis saw the crystal skull he knew he had to have it, possess it. He moved forward, the eyes of the skull drawing him across the room.

'*Por el amor di Dios, Señor!*'

A kneeling figure detached itself from darkness, rose suddenly in his path. Wide-sleeved arms were beseechingly raised, black smothering wings . . .

Don Luis, his attention still on the skull, jammed his pistol into a plump belly and distractedly pulled the trigger. The exploding priest smashed against a wall, sank like a deflating pigskin.

Gazing upwards, beneath the altar, Don Luis holstered the smoking gun. In a room strewn with the dead, he reached up, stretching out both hands reverently to touch the grinning face of Death.

CHAPTER ONE

There was something hanging from the tree and it wasn't apples. It wasn't the most welcoming sight in the world either. Buzzards had done unpleasant things to the face and body and so had the flies and dozens of other small eaters of men. Guts, black and withered, coiled downwards from the gaping belly like lengths of frayed rope. Sloane glanced at the hanging man as he rode by the lynching tree and he knew he was nearing the end of his journey; he'd reached civilisation.

It had been a long hard trail, a vengeance trail, taken up many years before when a gang of killers had butchered his parents. The killers had enjoyed their work and they'd taken their time doing it. When they'd finished with them, Jim and Martha Sloane welcomed death like an old friend.

Their only son was left to die in a white hell of desert. It was there that the boy had been found by Chang Fung, a one-armed Chinaman who had fled his troubled homeland to start up a citrus farm in California. Chang Fung raised the boy as his own, initiating him into the techniques of *Wu-shu*, the Chinese Arts of War. He'd been a good teacher and his adopted son an eager student. As he learned the ways of defending himself and destroying others, Sloane thought about how the martial arts were going to help him avenge his parents. Chang Fung had tried to talk him out of his thirst for vengeance, warning him not to dishonour the ancient Chinese teachings by using them for a selfish purpose. But the day came when Sloane decided he'd learnt all the old man had to teach and he saddled up and rode out to find the men who'd killed his Ma and Pa. It had taken him a long time but he'd done it. And, one by one, he'd killed them all with his bare hands.*

Now, at last, he was riding home, his mind filled with warm thoughts of Chang Fung, his wife, Hsiao Yu, and their daughter Su Fan. Especially Su Fan. She was slim and beautiful, her long black hair framing a pretty face in which laughing green eyes sparkled like jade. Her skin was honey and her lips tasted as sweet. Sloane and Su Fan had gotten to know each other well, better than brother and sister are supposed to. Especially on those days that Chang Fung and Hsiao Yu had taken the wagon into town to fetch supplies. Many times they'd lain together in the damp silence after love, their bodies pressed together, silver on gold. Since the orgy of violence in which he had destroyed his parents' killers, Sloane felt an emptiness inside him. Where before there had burnt a fierce consuming hatred, now there was emptiness, a void. Sloane hoped that Su Fan's love would fill that void.

On the trail ahead, a cluster of low timber buildings with a corral out back came into view. A stage-stop, Sloane realised, where horses were traded for a fresh team. There was also a small general store where local homesteaders picked up their supplies. Sloane was glad to see the store. He was low on meat and coffee. And they might have canned peaches. Chang Fung had an unquenchable fondness for canned peaches.

The store-keeper looked up from the pyramid of air-tights he was fussily constructing when the door opened and the stranger walked in.

'Howdy, mister,' he welcomed, rubbing plump hands on his overalls. 'What's your pleasure?'

As he spoke he roamed his eyes over the newcomer. The stranger was in his twenties, tall and loose-limbed. The long-coated suit he wore was tattered and trail-dusted; by its

* See *Sloane* by Steve Lee.

16

appearance, a veteran of many rough and tumbles. It was hard to tell but it seemed as if its colour might once have been white.

The face beneath the low-brimmed hat looked like it had seen its share of action too. Weather-worn, grooved with ancient scars, it was a map of experience, not all of it pleasant. The cheek-bones were high, the jaw firm-set. But it was the eyes that commanded attention. They were denim-blue, and cold and clear as ice. The frosty eyes settled on the pyramid of air-tights.

'Gimme two cans of them peaches ... and a cut of jerky.' There was an unhurried authority in the soft-spoken words.

'Yes-sir,' said the store-keeper, moving to fix the order.

'You got any coffee?' the stranger asked.

'Arbuckles ... We only carry the best.'

'I'll take some of that too.'

As he hacked at the dried beef, the store-keeper asked the same friendly everyday questions he always asked and got in return something less than the usual answers. He deduced that the stranger wasn't a talking man.

'You seen our dancin' Mex?' he asked, easing into a new line of conversation.

'I seen him,' said the stranger.

The store-keeper laughed, the laugh of someone who reckons they've got a problem licked.

'Reckon that'll keep them raiders away if'n they show up round here. They see him danglin' there an' they'll piss in their goddam boots. They'll know what we got waitin' fer 'em!'

'Raiders?' The stranger was leafing through a thick catalogue of eastern goods. His voice betrayed little interest.

'Sure, ain't you heard? There's a whole danged passel o' them murderin' pepper-guts ... There's some say they's worse than Murieta's gang ever was!'

The store-keeper shook his bald head in amazement. 'Beats me how you could've missed hearin' 'bout 'em ... Why, they been killin' an' massacreein' and runnin' off horses an' wimmen and the Lord knows what else besides!' The store-keeper paused in his impassioned revelations, looking sharp at the stranger. 'Say, where you headed anyhow?'

'West ... Down Orange way.'

'*Alone?*' The store-keeper's voice was edged with surprise.

The stranger nodded. The store-keeper laid both hands on the counter, a sudden movement, and leaned urgently towards the other man.

'Mister, that's where they been doin' all their killin' – you go down there, you're gonna ride straight into 'em!'

The stranger met the other man's anxiety with an unblinking stare. He said nothing. The heavy catalogue crashed down onto the counter.

The store-keeper followed the stranger out of his store, but not with the same haste. He knew about horseflesh and he looked appreciatively at the leggy Morgan the stranger mounted.

'What about your grub ... your coffee an' peaches?' he shouted, raising an arm up against the sun.

'Guess you've gone and ruined my appetite!' Sloane threw back as he rode out and the next instant the store-keeper was choking on his dust.

CHAPTER TWO

When Sloane reached the citrus plantation the red fingers of dawn were groping blindly through the trees after him. He'd ridden hard and fast all night, stopping only once to rest his lathered mount. His muscles felt leaden with weariness but apprehension of what he might find stoked his nerves to quivering readiness and chased the fog from his brain. He rode through the silent shadowy groves, smelling again the familiar delicate scent of the small orange-like fruit Chang Fung called satsumas. Behind their sweet fragrance he detected a harsher odour: the stench of charred wood and worse.

It was as he feared. The timber farmhouse he had helped build in days of laughter and song was a dark lifeless shell wisped by dregs of smoke. The flames had chased all colour from the ruin before themselves expiring. All that remained was stark and black and twisted – as if the house itself had died in screaming pain.

Sloane slipped down from the Morgan, horror dragging his movements. The smoke and the stench clogged his nostrils, pulled on his stomach. He stared into the black silence of the dead house. *Again!*

The years seemed to flow away, dissolving like the smoke spiralling about him, and he was twelve years old again and seeing his home after a gang of crazed killers had paid a visit. He felt the same numb shock of disbelief, the same sense of crippled grief, of hopeless, incomprehending despair. Like a hollow man whose soul has been jerked suddenly from his body, Sloane moved through the smoke, treading hot ash and fragments of life.

He found Hsiao Yu first. He recognised her from the

tatters of clothing that remained clinging to the black, dead flesh. There was nothing in the faceless bundle to remind him of a human being full of joy and laughter, the gentle loving woman who had reared him as her own.

Sloane reached out a hand, hesitant. Crisped flesh crumpled at his touch and he drew back, an ugly sound in his throat. Sickened, he turned and lurched away.

A few feet from the burnt-out house he found Chang Fung. The old Chinaman lay where he had died fighting for his home and family. His death had not been enough to satisfy the killers. Deep wounds, savagely inflicted, mutilated his face and body. He had not died alone. Sloane saw enough heads, limbs and other bits and pieces littered around to make four whole Mexicans when put together. The sight gave him a crazed kind of satisfaction. He looked for the sword with which Chang Fung had fought his last battle. It was gone.

Sloane stood tight-fisted above the bloodied carcass of his dead teacher. Grief and frustrated anger swelled up inside him. His body shook with fury. A wild *spirit cry* ripped from his throat and at the same instant he lashed out with his foot at a fire-chewed timber nearby. The wood fragmented into powdered smoke, scattering a hail of dying sparks.

There was still one body to find, the discovery he dreaded most. He stumbled through the boiling smoke, kicking aside the debris, searching, searching.

'*Su Fan!*' he screamed and the whippoorwills in the trees paused for the briefest moment before continuing their lamentations.

There was no other reply. He did not find the body of the girl he loved. He hoped she was safe in town. If the killers had taken her with them, she was better off dead.

Sloane leaned his body against a tree, grief pulling him down. He felt numb and empty, drained of *Tch'i*, the precious body energy that gave strength to his Kung Fu. Chang Fung had tried to teach him the Buddhist philosophy of non-attachment: without desire there is no loss. But desire is human and the loss weighed heavy. He blamed himself. Chang Fung had warned him that the gods punish those that misuse the martial arts for their own purposes. Sloane had not listened. He'd taken the Way of the Ruthless Man. He'd ridden out on his mission of vengeance leaving Chang Fung and Hsiao Yu and Su Fan unprotected. And it was them that the gods had struck down. *That* was his punishment.

Sloane felt cursed. Everything he loved had been torn from him like petals from a flower. He knew he was being punished for taking the Way of the Ruthless Man – yet with each punishment he grew more defiant, more ruthless. He refused to be humble and bow his head and accept the deaths of those he loved. He would fight back the way he knew best, the only way he knew: with his fists and his feet. He would track down the killers, the instruments of punishment, and destroy them as he had done others before. Let the gods blast him with their wrath, let *Kuan Ti*, the god of martial arts, deliver more cruel kicks of fate. It did not matter. He would not be stopped. It would end as it had begun. In bloody vengeance.

These thoughts chased through Sloane's brain like hungry howling dogs, yet even as he dwelt on his revenge, his senses remained alert. The unease tugging at the back of his mind became concrete sounds – the soft tread of feet on earth, the whisper of a man's body against brushing leaves. Sloane listened to the man creeping near-silently through the bushes towards him. He waited, apparently frozen in deep thought – then, as the creeping man stepped out behind him, he rose swiftly to his feet and pivoted, his right foot rising for a high kick. A kick that should have cracked against the side of the man's head. Instead, the other swiped aside his attack with a skilful arm-block and the same instant a dragon's-head fist smacked into his jaw.

Sloane hit the ground before he had time to feel surprised. Instantly, he rolled back onto his feet and sprang into a defensive horse stance. He faced his opponent. The man before him was a slender Chinaman in denim pants and a loose-fitting black shirt. He was young, in his early twenties, his handsome face tight with concentration. The two men sized each other up, their outstretched arms weaving like snakes.

Sloane launched his attack with a leopard punch to the head. The Chinaman slapped the blow aside with a swift *bon-sau*, at the same time pecking at Sloane's face with a vicious crane's beak. Sloane danced out of reach then came back quickly with a roundhouse strike. The Chinaman moved to meet it, breaking the kick with a body block that sent Sloane sprawling.

When he'd regained his feet, Sloane eyed the Chinaman with greater respect. The man was obviously a well-trained and versatile fighter, skilled in the martial arts. Sloane felt his body rising to the challenge, casting aside the tiredness and numbness that had slowed his movements. His *Tch'i* began to circulate freely once more, filling him with *nui gung*, the power of Inner Strength.

Behind a fast-punching flurry of blows, the Chinaman charged. Sloane blocked the assault, feigning a rake-hand attack. The Chinaman moved to counter. Sloane's other arm cleaved upwards, briefly smashing aside the Chinaman's defence. His whirling thunder kick exploded against the side of the Chinaman's head. Shaken, the young Chinaman reeled backwards. Then, with a cry of anger, he flung himself into a fierce flying kick. Sloane leapt up to meet him.

They clashed in mid-air, the impact flinging them apart, tossing them to the ground. Again they sprang into defensive stances and faced each other. With his tongue, the Chinaman licked at the blood at the corner of his mouth. His face cracked into a pained smile.

'Not bad, Mister Sloane,' he grudgingly admitted. 'Not bad at all.'

Sloane eyed him with suspicion. 'I don't know you,' he said.

'Chang Fung often spoke of you ... Su Fan too.'

'You knew them?'

The Chinaman looked over at the remains of the house, nodding his head grimly. 'I knew them ...' He turned back to Sloane. 'When you came at me Chinese-style, I figured it had to be you ... Never heard of no other Yankee could fight like that.'

He didn't speak like any Chinaman Sloane had ever heard. His voice was brisk and American-sounding, very different from Chang Fung's soft lilting way of talking. The Chinaman's face was youthful and fresh-looking. The brown eyes, large and lustrous, were ablaze with life. The high-arching brows above gave him an expression of permanent mild surprise. His hair was long and black, casually pushed to one side of a high-domed forehead. A thin moustache hung from beneath a straight nose, drooping down past thick lips towards a strong jaw.

It was the kind of face always ready with an easy smile, unusual in a fatalistic race like the Chinese. Right now grief was battling with the smile and the stalemate they'd reached made his face look uncomfortably rigid. For a brief moment the smile won out.

'William Wang is my name,' he announced. 'Billy to my friends.'

Sloane shook the hand offered him. 'You just get here?' he asked.

'No, I was here before ... Heard you comin' down the

trail and figured I'd hide out till I could see who it was. I was just gonna call out to you when you come at me like that...'

'Shouldn't creep up on a man that way,' said Sloane, 'not unless you're tired of living.'

Billy Wang slowly drew near to Chang Fung's butchered remains and shook his head. 'I can't believe it, Chang Fung and Hsiao Yu, both dead ... They were like a mother and father to me.'

Sloane stared at the young Chinaman. 'You *lived* here?' There was disbelief in his voice.

'That's right,' Billy answered. 'I guess if I hadn't gone into town yesterday I'd be lyin' there like that ... cut to pieces!'

Sloane grabbed the Chinaman with sudden urgency, wrapping his fingers in Billy's shirt, pulling him close.

'And Su Fan?' he demanded. 'Did she go into town with you? Where is she?'

Billy stepped back, tugging free of Sloane's grip. He turned his back on Sloane, breathing hard, his head lowered. Another time he might have felt anger but at that moment all his anger was already spoken for.

'She was here when I left,' he said flatly. He kicked out with his foot. The disembowelled body of a Mexican received the kick.

'Those bastards must've taken her with them!'

'It sure does look that way,' said Sloane.

Billy swung back towards him, his features fired with resolution. 'I'll get her back!' he promised. 'I'll find her and bring her back if it takes me the rest of my life ...'

'I wasn't plannin' on company,' said Sloane softly.

Billy's face changed. He stared at Sloane, a sudden wariness in his expression. 'No need for you to come,' he said. 'I can find her by myself. And take care of those murderin' bastards ...'

'I'm goin' after her,' Sloane said evenly. 'Don't matter none to me if I go alone or you come with me – but I'm goin'.'

Billy thought about it for a while, his face working hard. 'All right,' he decided. 'We'll both go.'

Sloane made no sign of pleasure at the news. He looked back down at the body of Chang Fung. 'Right now, looks like we got us some diggin' to do . . .'

They buried Chang Fung and his wife out in the tangerine groves, beneath the first tree they'd ever planted there. The bodies would give nourishment to the trees, Sloane realised. As the old Chinaman would have wished. All his life he had believed in the eternal balance of nature, the timeless cycle of Yin and Yang. In death he would continue to be a part of it : death giving birth to life.

Looking down at the bare graves, Sloane remembered how Chang Fung and his family had buried his own parents after they'd been murdered. Chang Fung had said fine words to speed their souls safely on the journey to the next life. Sloane struggled in his head to find words that would do the same for Chang Fung and Hsiao Yu.

Billy Wang did not have the ink or rice-paper to write out the necessary prayers for a proper Buddhist burial ceremony. As a boy he'd once been taught a spell to chase evil spirits away from the dead. He tried to remember it now. For a time they stood there in silence beneath the blossom-heavy trees. Then Sloane moved away, tugging on his hat, pulling the brim down low over his frosty eyes.

'Let's get after 'em,' he said.

CHAPTER THREE

They stopped by in town to pick up supplies for the journey ahead and to report the deaths to the sheriff. The tired-faced lawman showed little surprise at the news. Too many similar stories had already reached him, stories of murder, rape and horse-thieving.

'Seems there's this bandit chief down in Baja got it in his head he's gonna scare us into givin' California back to Mexico,' the sheriff informed them between mouthfuls of egg and beans.

'Calls hisself *El Muerte* ... That's Spik-talk for Death ... Not a bad choice a' name seein' as how he's gone and butchered the Willoughbys and Deke Wallace 'n' his boys and a coupla dozen others on top!'

'You sending a posse out after him?' Billy asked.

The sound the sheriff made was too rueful to be called a laugh. He jabbed his fork in the direction of the young Chinaman.

'Boy, I ain't fixin' to go down in no history books as the sheriff who lost half the menfolk in his town chasin' after a crazy Mexican bandit ... That killer's got thirty, forty guns ridin' with him, maybe more and that kinda trouble's a job for the Cavalry not the sheriff of a small town like this!' He shook his head, appalled by the very idea of it. 'And if he skips back across the border, which he sure-as-Hell will do if he's got any sense under that sombrero a' his, then even them bluecoats is gonna be left standin' there at the frontier a'whistlin' *Dixie* with him wavin' to 'em from the other side.'

The sheriff clattered his fork down onto the empty plate and settled back to pick his teeth with a thumbnail.

'No, sir,' he concluded, 'any man that goes up against a vicious sonovabitch killer like this here El Muerte's just gotta be one dang-blasted fool!'

A short time later, two such fools left town riding south towards the border.

The trail left by El Muerte and his gang was not a difficult one to follow ... Burnt-out ranches, looted wagons and the abused, stiffening corpses of whole families and solitary travellers marked their passing.

Sloane and Billy Wang also saw the hanging bodies of many Mexicans along the trail, luckless victims of the wave of fear and hatred that followed in the wake of the bandits. Prejudice was a barrel of explosives at any time and now El Muerte had lit the fuse that could blast the State apart. Seeing the suspicion in the faces of those they passed on the trail, Sloane grew glad his companion was a Chinaman and not a Mexican.

Most of the time they rode in silence, the silence of hooves on sand, creaking saddles and men deep in thought. The silence worried Sloane. Not because he was a talking man, which he wasn't, but because he knew Billy had too much youth and enthusiasm for life in him to be that quiet unless there was something he was keeping back. Something Sloane should know. He made an assault on the barrier of unspoken words.

'How'd you come to be with Chang Fung?' he asked.

'It was my uncle's idea,' Billy replied. 'My Uncle Wu that is – he's a hatchet man for the Red Spears Tong in 'Frisco – Well, he was an old friend of Chang Fung's and when you left, Uncle Wu heard about it and figured maybe Chang Fung could use some help. So he sent me out here ... I jumped at the chance ... Uncle Wu is so old-fashioned; he goes in for pig-tails and dressing up and ceremonies and all that old Chinese stuff ... Me, I'm a first generation

27

American and I was glad to get out here where the action is.

'Well, I guess I was till this happened,' he added with less enthusiasm.

'I always wanted to meet Chang Fung. I'd heard tell he was a master of Chinese boxing, even though he only had one arm. He was just as good as people said he was – a great fighter and a good teacher too.'

Sloane nodded in agreement, remembering the years of gruelling practice at Kung Fu, the many painful exercises Chang Fung had forced on him as a boy because he wanted his pupil to attain that perfection which not even he had succeeded in reaching.

'He could do tricks Uncle Wu never even heard of,' Billy continued. 'There was this one trick he did – maybe you've heard of it – the Grand Ultimate Kick?'

'I've heard,' said Sloane.

'It's so secret most people don't even believe it exists. But Chang Fung knew the secret. I've heard tell he was the only man outside China who knew it. He told me he was gonna show it me some day when I was ready. But he never got round to it.' Billy shook his head, regretful. 'Now I guess I'll never know the secret.'

'He ever say anythin' . . . 'bout me?' Sloane asked. He'd been thinking about the question for some time.

Billy looked uncomfortable. 'Chang Fung was ... Well, he was kind of old-fashioned too, you know,' he said awkwardly. 'He had this big thing about filial devotion. Well, a lot of the old folks do. They all think a son should do what his father says even when it don't make no sense. I guess he kind of looked on you as his son and when you left the way you did, he got pretty sore at you. Guess he thought you was ungrateful or something . . .'

'I prob'ly was,' said Sloane. He made it sound as if he meant it.

'There's somethin' else you should know too, Sloane,' said Billy in a voice promising bad news. 'I didn't want to tell you this back there at the house but . . .'

Sloane waited, his face impassive as the scrub-studded wasteland through which they rode.

'Well, it's like this. After you left Su Fan didn't know if you were ever comin' back again. Well, she and me, we were planning on getting married . . .'

'*Married!*' Sloane repeated the word. It fell from his lips like a hot stone. His hands tightened on the reins, became white, knuckled fists, tightly clenched.

He turned his face from Billy's, his eyes narrowing, searching the vast plains for something, he didn't know what. His eyes fixed on a distant mountain range but his gaze was inward-turned. The mountains were remote, grey, massive, unfeeling. A man could spend a lifetime swinging an axe at a mountain and never hurt it Sloane thought enviously.

'That's why I didn't think you should come along,' Billy went on. 'If you want to turn back now, I'll understand . . .'

'No,' said Sloane, his voice almost casual, 'I got other reasons than Su Fan for findin' El Muerte . . .'

'The old man and woman . . . ?'

'Chang Fung said to me once – "A man may not live under the same sky as his father's killer!"'

Billy raised a nervous laugh. 'That sounds like my Uncle Wu. Or a fortune cookie!'

The laughter died in Billy's throat when he saw Sloane's expression. It was dark as a storm-threatening sky.

'You understand, don't you?' Billy appealed. 'About Su Fan, I mean?'

'Sure, I understand,' said Sloane in a voice completely empty of understanding.

It was many miles before either of them spoke again.

It was their fifth day on the trail and the sun was dragging itself down towards the foothills like a wounded animal leaving a bloody trail across the sky. Sloane sniffed the dry air, the suspicion of woodsmoke becoming a certainty.

'Probably some saddle-tramp brewing himself a pot of coffee,' Billy suggested.

'Maybe, maybe not,' said Sloane.

He nudged the Morgan with his heels, urging the horse towards a point in the distance where a thin column of smoke curled lazily upwards. Billy hesitated a moment, then followed on the pinto.

The smoke drew them to a shallow-bottomed arroyo snaking across the plains like a knife-wound gouged deep into the earth's dry flesh. They rode into the arroyo, following the boulder-strewn track that unwound raggedly before them. After a few minutes they cleared a sharp bend in the gulley and found themselves looking at the source of the smoke – a neat campfire atop of which eggs spluttered in a pan of grease. A chestnut mare stood ground nearby, muzzling a clump of salt-grass. She raised her head at the intruders, favouring them with a jaundiced look. There was no sign of her owner.

'Where d'you think he's gone?' Billy asked as they drew slowly near to the fire.

'Nowhere,' said Sloane, climbing down from his horse. He strolled over to the fire, feeling hungry.

Billy followed, looking anxiously about, turning full circle as he walked. There were plenty of boulders around but none of them large enough to hide a man.

'I don't see him,' Billy announced.

'But he sees you . . .'

Sloane cupped both hands to his mouth and raised an upwards-leaping shout – 'Come on down or we'll start without you!'

Above them, on the rim of the arroyo, a man suddenly appeared.

'Grab a cloud – both of you!' he yelled with the authority of a man behind a .44 Henry rifle.

Sloane cast an appraising glance at the rust-coloured sky. 'There ain't no clouds,' he observed.

'Then you better reach a mite higher an' see if you kin find one quick!' returned the man with the rifle.

Sloane and Billy obligingly raised their hands heavenwards. The man with the rifle slid-scrambled down the sandy wall of the arroyo. He moved towards them, rifle-ready.

'Now don't you be tryin' nothin',' he warned, ''cause old Henry here'll open you up, easy as spit . . .'

He stooped and with his free hand took the pan of eggs off the fire.

'*Hell!*'

Pan and eggs hit the dirt. The man blew on scorched fingers, keeping Sloane and Billy covered the while.

Whichever way you looked at him, upwards or sidewise, he was a big man, big and clumsy-looking as the Walker Colt on his hip. Sloane guessed him to be nearer fifty than forty but his wide shoulders and the way he carried himself suggested there was a lot of fight left in him yet. His face was more jaw than anything else. Rugged as an Indian rock carving, it was a face that looked like it had gotten in the way of trouble with painful regularity. Only a life-time of fistfights could have shaped such a face, Sloane decided. The eyes in the face were grey and honest-straight with a mellow sadness in them that spoke of too many disappointments. The grey eyes seized on Billy Wang.

'Great God-a-Mighty – a Chinaman! As if murderin' Mexicans wasn't bad enough, we've now got the Yellow Peril roamin' free to boot!' The rifle-barrel and the man behind it veered from Billy to Sloane. 'And the other one a penniless drifter by the look a' him . . . Now there's as suspicious a combination as ever I seen!' The man had a slow drawling manner of speaking with as much of Dublin in it as Dallas.

'Now perhaps you'll tell me what you mean by breakin' in on a man's dinner uninvited?'

'We didn't mean no harm,' Billy threw back. 'We thought you might've been in trouble!'

'And what kind of trouble would that be that I'd be needin' help from the likes of you two?'

'Bandit trouble,' said Sloane.

'What would you be knowin' 'bout that?' the big man asked, his voice tightening a notch.

'Just that you've been trailin' them for as long as we have, maybe longer.'

The big man considered the men at the end of his gun-barrel anew, as if he'd seriously misjudged them. His searching gaze lit on the three big metal stars which studded Sloane's belt.

'Is it lawmen you are?' he asked.

'No,' said Sloane. 'Two men with a score to settle.'

'What kind of a score?'

'A blood score.'

'The only kind worth havin',' the big man acknowledged. He lowered his rifle and the other two lowered their hands.

'Looks as if I'm owin' you boys an apology.'

'Forget it,' said Sloane. 'A careful man lives longer.'

'Amen to that, Mister —?'

'Sloane.'

'Joe's the name, Joe Hardy.'

Sloane matched the man's hand and shook it.

'That's a powerful strong hand you got there, Mister Sloane. Reckon I'd rather be shakin' it than feelin' it on m' jaw.'

Billy Wang stepped forward and made himself known.

'A pleasure to meet you, Billy. And now perhaps I can interest you gentlemen in a plate a' grub an' some coffee?'

As they ate, Sloane and Billy told Joe about Chang Fung and Hsiao Yu and how they were aiming on getting back Su Fan.

'It's a cruel world to be sure,' Joe sympathised. 'But yer no doubt wonderin' for what reason it is that I am meself on the trail a' this mangy polecat, El Muerte. Well, he's got somethin' a' mine too, somethin' dear to me heart. Only it ain't a woman, God forbid, but a horse.'

Joe sensed the surprise his guests tried to conceal.

'That's right, lads, a horse! And no ord'nary horse neither but the prettiest most golden palamino that ever raised hoofs to the moon.'

'Sounds like quite a horse,' laughed Billy.

'That it is . . . Why if you was to see that horse runnin' in the wind, proud as a peacock with its mane all flowin' behind, you'd think you was watchin' a sun-beam come down from Heaven above to play on God's own Earth.'

'No horse is worth dyin' for,' said Sloane bluntly, helping himself to a third cup of coffee from the pot.

Joe Hardy looked across the fire at the unshaven man in the dirty white suit. The man was young, half his age, but there was a hardened sureness in the cold blue eyes meeting his that made Joe feel like a child. He lowered his gaze to the dancing flames between them, more quickly than he would have liked.

'Well, maybe you're right there, Mister Sloane,' he allowed. 'Maybe there's more to it than the horse.'

He pulled a cigar from the top pocket of his leather vest and lit it from the fire. It seemed to give him encouragement to open up.

'Well, boys, it's like this,' he began. 'You see afore you a man who's spent his life chasin' a pot a' gold. And everytime I've gotten near that pot a' gold, I've reached out an' grabbed for it and taken it in me arms – and always it's turned out to be a crock a' shit!'

Joe looked round for reactions. There was a suspicion of a smile in Sloane's eyes and Billy Wang was grinning like a loon.

'Laugh you may,' Joe chided, 'but it's the God's honest truth an' that's how it's always been with me. It's damn near the story of me life!'

He contemplated the gray smoke wafting from his cigar for a moment before launching deeper into his story.

'Y'see, I came over from the Old Country when I was but a young lad with empty pockets an' a head full a' dreams. I was a worker though an' fightin' mad to succeed. In no time at all I'd found meself a wife and a patch a'land to call me own. Oh, I was a proud man in them days – I had everythin' a man could wish for includin' a son.'

Joe's face lit up in a warm smile of happy memories. Then the smile froze, flawed by sadness. The sadness eroded the smile from his face. He took a deep puff on his cigar and the smoke billowed out in a sigh.

'Yes, an' then it started . . . Sickness took our little Tyrone from us an' Kathleen soon after, an' Injuns burned our cabin to the ground an' with it everythin' in the world I owned. I looked round for a way of workin' meself back up again. In them days everybody was lookin' for *gold*. It was like a fever. I joined in the rush an' got meself a good-sized claim – or so I thought till me thievin' Judas of a partner jumped the claim. Then I tried me hand at sheep-rearin'. Cattlemen slaughtered me flock, so I became a cattleman meself. Rustlers ran off with the herd . . . and so it went on, just one run a' rotten bad luck after another. Then I set meself up as a horse-breeder an' I was doin' so well at it I thought f'sure me luck had changed – an' then along comes this El Muerte an' helps himself to me best horses. Well, that was it I can tell you, the straw that broke the camel's back! Now I reckon every man's got his own Alamo inside a' him, that moment when he says to himself that he's taken all the crap he's goin' to an' the time has come to make his stand even if it's his last!'

'This is your stand, right?' Billy asked.

'Damn right it is! Oh, I'm very fond a' that golden pala-mino – it's a fine horse an' with my own bare hands I helped bring him into this world, God help me. But no, it's not just the horse, it's more the principle a' the matter! So I'm ridin' out to find this bandit feller an' when I find him I'm goin' to walk up to him like a man an' say, "Thank you very much, Mister El Muerte, sir, for lookin' after me horse for me, but now, if it's all the same to you, I'll be takin' him back off of you!'

'Maybe he'll be of a mind to keep the horse,' said Sloane.

'In that case there's two things likely to happen – he can kill me or I can kill him . . . And if it's me that has to go, well, I can't think of a finer way for a man to die than with his boots on fightin' for what he believes in – like Davey Crockett an' a lot of other grand lads at the Alamo. It would be a noble gesture, to be sure, a magnificent gesture!'

'I'd sure like to be there and see his face when you ask him for the horse back,' said Billy grinning.

'Well, now, me fine yeller lad, why don't you be comin' along with me an' you can ask him for your woman back at the same time?'

Billy's head lifted in surprise. 'I don't know about that . . .' Uncertain, he looked over for Sloane's opinion.

'Why not?' said Sloane carelessly. 'The more the merrier.'

'Then it's settled!' Joe exclaimed, slapping his thigh. 'Three against forty instead a' one against forty – why the odds is in our favour already!'

CHAPTER FOUR

Sloane and Billy rose with the dawn to go through the routine of Kung Fu exercises each of them practised daily. The series of exercises they followed had been designed to keep men mentally alert and their bodies at the peak of physical condition. Properly carried out the exercises would also increase their speed and help perfect their fighting skill. The two men practised alone, unaware of anything but their own striving towards perfection. Each knew his abilities as a fighter were going to be tested as they had never been before. A weak kick or a clumsy fall could no longer be tolerated. A mistake during a work-out meant a moment's shame. In the battles ahead it would mean certain death.

Joe watched their sweeping arms, their leaps and jumps and their whirling kicks – high-reaching as a can-can dancer in a saloon. He threw back his head and hooted with amusement.

'I never was a dancin' man meself but I don't mind seein' a bit of a jig,' he laughed. 'Too bad I don't have me fiddle with me or I'd give you a tune to set the feet a'flyin', f'sure!' Clapping his hands and beating one foot on the ground, Joe launched into a spirited rendering of an old Irish jig.

Ignoring his laughter, their faces fierce with concentration, Sloane and the Chinaman continued their exercises, flowing through the intricate patterns of movement with practised grace. Faster than Joe could follow, their fists flew out and pummelled the air and their kicks scythed through whole armies of imaginary enemies. To Joe it looked like the grandest barn-dance ever.

For forty minutes they followed the elaborate sets of exercises developed hundreds of years before by priests who had lived the other side of the world. The techniques of Kung Fu had been devised by the priests of the Shaolin Temple in Honan Province, China with two purposes in mind. First as a reliable means of self-defence for weaponless monks in times of war and disorder. Second as a way of complete integration of mind and body. In their wisdom the priests realised that it was worthless to sit cross-legged all day in devout meditation if the body was wasting away from lack of use. So they developed Kung Fu, a system which demanded a healthy body as well as an agile mind. And in the combination of the two displayed by skilled masters of Kung Fu, the monks discovered a sublime harmony, a harmony that expressed the perfect balance of the creative life forces more potently than any prayer.

Had those priests been able to watch Sloane and Billy as they practised their martial artistry in an arid sun-splashed wasteland, they would undoubtedly have nodded their heads in approval, for both men had attained a rare degree of skill. But they would have been shocked at the use to which the two men intended to put their skill. The Shaolin monks preferred to turn and run from danger rather than abuse their great power. They never hurt another human being unless it was completely unavoidable and even then only with the greatest reluctance and remorse. It was forbidden by their Buddhist religion and their code of conduct. The art of Kung Fu was a noble one, devised for gradual self-development. Not for bloody slaughter.

'And what was all that about – leapin' around like a couple a' flamin' monkeys in a cage?' Joe wanted to know when his new-found companions joined him for a cup of the molasses-thick brew he dared to call coffee.

A smile flickered at the edges of Sloane's mouth. 'Had ants in my pants,' he explained.

Billy shot him a glance of amused reproach then looked over at Joe. 'Kung Fu,' he said as if those two words cleared up everything. Joe's gnarled face took on a look of even greater bafflement.

'And what in Heaven's name is that when it's at home?' he demanded.

'Chinese boxing,' Billy revealed, grinning. 'The best kind there is.'

Joe drew himself upright, suddenly indignant. 'Oh, it is is it?' he asked in a bantering tone. 'Well, let me tell you, young feller, that I've been in a scrap or two meself an' I reckon these fists a' mine . . .' He raised his big-knuckled hands, clenching them fiercely for Billy's benefit. '. . . can give as good a punch as the next man – whether he's a Chinaman or a bloody Hindoo!'

Billy's laughter got him even more hotted up.

'And I'd like to see the Chinaman alive that could go five rounds with Big Jim Murphy a' New York – or any other fightin' Irishman worth the name!'

'Chinese boxing's different,' Billy laughed. 'A man who knows Kung Fu don't have need of any weapons other than his hands and feet. He can take on anybody or anything and usually wins.'

'Is that a fact?' Joe growled scornfully.

'It sure is!' Billy affirmed. 'Ask Sloane here.'

Joe looked over at Sloane.

'It's a fact,' Sloane allowed.

'Shame on you for sidin' with a heathen!' said Joe reproachfully, reaching over for his rifle. He pulled the Henry towards him and cradled it in his lap, fondly patting the stock.

'I should like to see how your Kung Phooey stands up against one a' these,' he chuckled, 'that I would! I know which one my money'd go on. Why many's the time I'd have been a goner for sure if it weren't for Old Henry here, many's the time! When El Muerte an' his murderin' crew came ridin' straight at me, for one!'

Suddenly Sloane was interested in the conversation. 'You've seen El Muerte?'

Pinned down by Sloane's gaze, Joe shifted uncomfortably. 'Well, yes and no, in a manner a' speakin' . . . The truth of it is that, in my eyes, one greaser looks much of a likeness to another, an' there bein' a whole heap of 'em comin' at me with guns a'blazin', I didn't hang around to ask no names . . . but there was this one big fella who could've been El Muerte an' him I'd know again f'sure if I saw him. An' there's a couple a' the others walkin' round with me lead in 'em or Henry here wasn't doin' his stuff!' He patted the rifle with tender emphasis.

'Just the same,' said Billy, 'when it comes to my life I'd sooner trust my own hands to get me out of trouble than a metal stick that could jam up on me any time . . .'

'Oh, you would now would you?' Joe asked, a sudden crafty gleam appearing in his eyes. 'Well, if you turn yourselves round slowly, an' I mean *slowly*, you might see something to make you change your mind . . .'

Sloane and Billy turned. Slowly. They heard it before they saw it – a mean-looking diamondback rattler nearly six feet long, sliding rapidly over the sand towards them. It had the smell of coffee in its flat ugly nose and it was sore as hell it hadn't been invited over for a cup.

The snake reared up within striking distance of Sloane and Billy, its vicious tongue-flicking head weaving from side to side as if it were making its mind up which of the two men to bite first. Billy sat paralysed, rooted to the spot, as he watched the deadly snake inching towards him. There was no man alive he was afraid to tackle with his bare hands and Kung Fu artistry. But a poison-fanged rattler was something else.

Sloane eyed the killer snake with the same unblinking intensity as it watched him. Taking deep but imperceptible breaths to keep his body calm, he judged the distance between him and the swaying, restless head. He weighed his own speed against that of the rattler's. There was a chance he could grasp its neck before the poison-teeth sank into him. It wasn't a very big chance but it was the only one he had. Sloane tensed to make his move.

The sudden shattering blast ripped the snake's head from its body. The head leapt into the air and landed ten feet away, tongue still flickering. The headless body swerved drunkenly from side to side, searching for its lost head. Then it slumped to the ground and, like ripples in a water-barrel, slowly uncoiled.

Sloane and the Chinaman turned to face Joe. The big man contentedly blew smoke from the tip of his rifle.

'Like I was sayin', boys,' he continued casually, savouring the moment, 'give me a rifle every time . . . I may not know nothin' 'bout no Chinese boxin' but I'd as soon have me finger on Old Henry's trigger when some bean-eatin' bandit's comin' at me with a Mexican boxin' glove – the kind with six inches a' cold sharp steel!'

They rode steadily south. Above them the sun grew hotter and harsher, and around them the land seemed to shrivel and die until it was like a dry, empty husk stretching lifelessly before them as far as the eye could reach. They passed fewer and fewer villages. When they did, dark bleak-eyed faces watched their passing from doorways, silently resentful. Sometimes lean barefoot packs of coffee-coloured children chased alongside with mocking Spanish insults. Joe scattered them with laughing blasts of anger.

Most of the time, Sloane rode ahead of his two companions, like a gaunt, aloof spectre guiding them purposefully into the death-lands. He preferred it that way. Alone he didn't have to mask the fierce blaze of hatred he felt inside. He wanted to nurture that hate, to feel it growing inside of him for the day when he would be face to face with Chang

40

Fung's killers. Then he would unleash it on them in a whirl-wind fury of vengeance.

There was another reason he preferred to ride up ahead. It meant he didn't have to listen to Joe airing his mouth all day long.

Joe had found a captive audience in Billy— 'Ah, Mexico! Now there's a savage place, f'sure – full a' wild beauty the likes a' which you've never seen I can promise you, Billy. And beautiful women too, beguilin' willin' women, dark an' plump as grapes and as sweet to the lips.'

'Swell,' said Billy, 'but there's only one woman I'm inter-ested in – the one we're gonna bring back.'

'Sure, I was forgettin' . . . But how can you be sure this girl a' your's is gonna be in one piece when you find her?'

Billy's face hardened. He'd given a lot of thought to what El Muerte and his men could do to Su Fan, had perhaps already done to her. He hated to think about it but the fears refused to go away. All he could do was clutch at a faint hope and hang on tight.

'She's a good-looking girl,' he said. 'Too good-looking for them to kill. . .'

'Maybe . . . but you never can tell with these Mexicans. They're a cruel race a' men – with tempers hot as chilli.'

'Anyhow,' Billy countered, 'How d'you know you'll get your horse back in one piece?'

Joe's laughter rang out across the emptiness through which they rode. 'Because it's a good-lookin' horse, me boy, an' because horses don't answer back none!' Joe's grin became a sly one as he looked over at the young Chinaman. 'You know, Billy, I feel it me duty to warn you that Mexicans are not very partial to a Chinaman, no, not partial to 'em at all. Take Murieta now, he'd get ahold a' half-a-dozen Chinamen an' tie 'em by their pig-tails with their heads all close to-gether like a bunch a' grapes – an' then he'd cut all a' their throats together with one slash a' his knife!' Joe stole a sidewise glance at Billy to judge the effects of his words. 'I hope I'm not alarmin' you none?' he asked.

'Nope, not a bit,' Billy replied impassively. 'Anybody try any of that stuff on me and I'll just tell 'em I'm an American citizen.'

'Will you now,' Joe chuckled. 'Well, I hope for your sake, Billy, that you'll be able to get the words out an' that you won't be chewin' on a Mexican sandwich at the time!'

'I've heard about that Mexican food – pretty damn hot, huh?'

'So it is,' Joe agreed, 'but that wasn't what I had in mind...'

'Well, what is this Mexican sandwich?' Billy snapped impatiently. He didn't like the way the big Irishman was playing with him.

Joe shook his head, smiling in the manner of someone who thinks he knows more than the next man. 'Billy,' he said, 'I don't know to what heathen idol it is that you address your prayers – but pray to it that you'll never be given the chance to find out!'

Billy got his chance the very next day.

They found a covered wagon lying across the trail, shattered and horseless. Three people had been travelling in the wagon. They were white and they were dead. Their possessions lay scattered around, along with all their hopes of a better life out west.

The woman was the first they found. She lay naked in the dust, the marks of violation scratched into her body. Her eyes stared sightlessly up at the sun, her expression moulded by terror. Her throat was a bloody gash from ear to ear. Nearby lay her child, a boy of eight or so. They'd cut his throat too.

Billy found the man round the other side of the wagon. He backed away from what he saw, vomit clawing up his throat.

They'd stretched out his arms and legs and pinned them to the ground. In his pain, he'd managed to tear free his right hand. His eyes had been gouged from their sockets and hung from his head on bloody threads. His nose and lips were clumsily cut away. His penis had been hacked off at the root and was stuffed in his mouth along with his testicles.

Billy stared at the ruined body. All he could think of was that the men responsible for what he saw had their hands on the girl he loved. The thought made him want to scream.

Sloane and Joe joined him and looked down at the thing before them that had been a man. The muscles in Sloane's face grew taut but he said nothing. He'd seen too much too often to show any reaction. But when the time came that he stood face to face with the killer who called himself El Muerte he would remember this nameless man and what they'd done to him and all the others like him.

Joe whistled softly and pushed his battered hat to the back of his head. 'I'll say this for that El Muerte,' he said, 'he sure knows how to serve up a Mexican sandwich!'

'*You bastard!*'

Billy threw himself at the big Irishman, his face suddenly crazed with anger. His right fist streaked towards the older man's face. The punch didn't connect. Billy found his hand wrapped firmly up in Sloane's fingers. Sloane pushed his hand aside.

'Leave it,' he warned, looking coolly into the Chinaman's face. 'Our business is with them that did this.'

'The men that did this have got Su Fan!' Billy hurled back at him.

Sloane stepped forward, narrowing the short distance between them. 'You think I could forget that?' he asked, his voice harsh and strained.

Billy didn't answer. They stared at each other in a wordless duel. Then Billy made a disgusted noise in his throat and swung away, turning his back on the others and heading back to the horses.

'Billy!' Joe hurried after him. 'It was a foolish thing I said back there, Billy,' he said when he'd caught up with him. 'Sloane should've let you take a poke at me . . .'

Billy turned to face him, his face still flushed with anger. He glared at the Irishman.

'Will you not forgive me, Billy? I guess we all have our ways a' hidin' things an' I reckon talkin' like that was mine . . .'

Billy took a deep breath, his face slowly relaxing. When Sloane joined them, the two men were shaking hands.

'They're still headed south,' he announced. 'Tomorrow we'll be in Mexico.'

CHAPTER FIVE

There was a US Cavalry patrol on one side of the border and a detachment of *Federales* on the other. The soldiers in both camps were bored. They thought of sleep and the good times they had had and the good times they would have again when they were not on patrol. Men such as these know nothing of darkness. They stick close to the small friendly areas captured by the yellow glare of their camp fires. They see the moon and the stars; nothing else. They do not see the scorpion scurrying past their feet nor the jaguar watching them like a shadow with eyes. Neither did they see Sloane and his companions as they stole silently past in the night.

The first town they came to was a lively little place called Tijuana. Hardly bigger than a village, the town made up in sinfulness what it lacked in size. It straddled the frontier like a voracious spider weaving a gaudy web to catch the gringos whose business or notoriety brought them to the Republic: the cattlemen and miners and outlaws running from a noose. It caught them, it hugged them and it sucked them dry. Its female citizens were much the same.

It was late when the three men rode in but the saloons and cantinas were filled with light and music that spilled over and across the wide busy plaza at the centre of the town. They eased their horses through the restless noisy crowd thronging the plaza. A man shouted to them as they passed, a dapperly dressed American caught up in a rare flush of patriotic feeling. Across the border he wouldn't have given them the time of day. Here he greeted them like life-long friends. He wore a curly-brimmed derby on his head and a plump black-eyed whore on each arm.

'You've come to the right place, boys!' he called. 'These

greaseritas sure know how to pleasure a man!' He planned on sharing more of his wisdom – but then he got a good look at their faces and he forgot what else he had to say. The whores laughed and flashed inviting smiles at the newcomers. Their benefactor tugged them towards a saloon, his patriotic desire for the companionship of fellow Americans taking second place to a sudden urge for whiskey. The girls went on looking back over their shoulders until they were swallowed by the crowd.

Joe licked his lips. 'How's about a drop a' somethin' to chase the dust from the throat?' he suggested. 'Some a' that Taos Lightnin' maybe?'

'Now what red-blooded, yellow-skinned young American could refuse an invitation like that?' said Billy eagerly.

Sloane's attention was elsewhere. He was watching the crowd. A band of *mariaches*, all in identical wide sombreros, passed close by. The strolling musicians were boisterously chanting the words to a repetitious song. The song was about the execution of Emperor Maximilian and it was a happy one. A lot of the crowd cheerfully joined in, adding their own voices and hand-clapping. They were still filled with joy at the victory over the French. If they had to have dictators, they preferred the home-grown kind like Juarez to the imported variety. Packs of dark hard-faced men weaved through the crowd. Sloane eyed them narrowly. They could have been *vaqueros* in town for a drunk or they could have been bandits. Bandits just returned from across the border.

'Careful what you say,' Sloane told the others. 'He may have friends here.'

The saloon they chose was called *El Cimarrón*. Beneath the painted name a smaller sign translated this as *The Crazy Horse Saloon*. They settled on it because it looked the kind of place where the men they were after might drink – more so than the big bright saloons where the Texans and Californios were being enthusiastically helped to part with their money.

46

Inside, the air was thick with the laughter of men being men and the curling fumes of tobacco and marijuana. They found themselves a corner table and sat. Sloane chose a place with his back to the wall from where he could see who was coming and who was going. His searching eyes swept the low-ceilinged room, pausing briefly at each group of oily faces bent over bottles and cards. The faces were copper-tinted beneath the yellow lamplight. They moved expressively as they talked and so did the hands held before them.

Their entrance into the saloon had not drawn much interest. Travel-stained gringos were not a rare sight in Tijuana and even a Chinaman was worth hardly more than a momentary stare and perhaps a nudge to a drinking *compadre*. Yet Sloane noted the men at one table glancing in their direction long after the interest of others had died. There were eight men at the table and they had the appearance, but not the humble manners, of peasants.

'Recognise any old friends?' Sloane asked Joe.

Like a conspirator hatching a plot, Joe leaned across the table closer to Sloane. He shook his head, his voice low. 'Nope, I had a quick look-see as we came in. But like I told you, they all look alike to me. Like Chinamen!' He tossed the last two words at Billy with a chuckle.

They drank tequila, helping the fiery liquid down their throats with fingers of salt and twists of lemon. By the end of the first jar even Billy had gotten a taste for it.

'Reminds me of saké,' he said. 'That's liquor made with rice.'

'If it gets you drunk, it can't be bad,' Joe philosophised.

They were starting on the second jar when a shadow fell across the table and stayed there. Sloane's eyes slid up the shadow. Before they reached the face at the end of it he knew it would be one of the men who had been watching them from the other table. He was right.

The Mexican standing uneasily by their table was as

47

humble-looking a fellow as Sloane had ever seen. He stood timidly by their table, his straw hat held nervously before him, his tanned face slightly bowed and full of uncertainty. When he spoke, his low whining voice was like the licking of a dog's tongue.

'*Perdóneme, Señores Nortes Americanos,*' he began, 'for daring to dishonour your table with my presence that is unwelcome to you. My friend Tomas over there said you would beat me for sure. He said to me – "Pancho Gonzalez . . ." – that is my name, señores – "Pancho Gonzalez," he said, "those nice Americanos over there, they just want to drink their tequila and have some fun. They do not want to speak to one such as you." And I say back to this Tomas – a good and honest man he is, señores, and a good father to his children. That is him you see over there, the one with the moustache . . .'

Over at the table of watching men, Tomas' moustache curled around a beaming grin. He raised a hand and wriggled three fingers in greeting.

Pancho Gonzalez continued: 'I say to him – "Tomas, *mi amigo*, have you ever seen Americanos with such kind friendly faces as those señores Americanos over there? If you say you have, you are a lying pig!" I tell him. Because those ones are not like other Americanos. They are very generous Americanos and in particular the one who looks so distinguished in the prime of his life . . .' Here Pancho paused briefly to favour Joe with an admiring smile. ' "Him I know by his handsome face to be a very good man", I say to Tomas. "He will not mind if I approach his table and speak with him and his *compañeros* . . ." '

'For God's sake, man, hurry and get it out,' Joe urged the Mex. 'What is it you want with us?'

'Pardon me, señores, for the slowness of my tongue, but I am a humble man and not at all used to speaking to such fine *caballeros* as yourselves. I was over there sharing a jar of

48

pulque with my compadres, all honest men as you can see, when you honoured us all by entering into this unworthy *cantina*. When I see you come in through the door, I say to Tomas and to Pablo too and to my other friends, I say, "What fine boots he has on his feet that big tall Americano that looks so handsome . . ." Is it not as I have said, Tomas, *muchacho mio*?'

For confirmation Pancho looked over to where his seven friends were sitting. All seven had been watching and listening with the very closest attention possible and each of them had a grin on his face as big as a slice of water melon. The one called Tomas stood straight up, the grin vanishing clean off his face. He was dressed, as were all his companions, in white cotton shirt and pants. He walked over and joined Pancho, holding his hat respectfully in his hands.

'Si, señores,' he gravely affirmed. 'He speaks no more than what is true.'

'Never before in my whole life have I seen such wonderful boots as these I tell myself,' Pancho went on. 'I say to Tomas and to Pablo and to the others, I say – "These are most definitely boots any man would be proud to wear. Look how soft is the leather, like the skin of a rich woman. And the heels thick and high like a big stack of gold pesos. Everyone in Tijuana would look up to a man who wore such magnificent boots as these – especially the *chicas*!"'

Pancho's dark eyes gleamed at the thought. The gleam in his eye made Joe shift his booted feet uncomfortably under the table. Then Pancho's head drooped as he lowered his gaze to his own feet and the eyes of everyone were drawn to the ragged sandals he wore, sandals so rotten and worn and full of holes that it appeared only by a miracle could they remain clinging to his dirt-encrusted feet. Pancho's face filled with anguish at the sight, anguish and incomprehension as if he could scarcely believe that it was his own feet he was looking at and not those of some hopeless and diseased beggar.

'How can a man have pride,' he asked, as if speaking directly to the Almighty, 'when he looks down and sees his feet in these stinking *huaraches* through which all men may see his toes?'

As proof of his words, Pancho furiously wiggled his toes which protruded like black stubs of mud from the grisly remains of his *huaraches*. Then he raised his eyes to Joe, a look of childlike eagerness taking possession of his face.

'When I see your boots, señor, I think to myself how fine it would be to feel those wonderful boots on my feet. And I say to Tomas and to Pablo and to my other *compañeros*, I say to them, that Americano with the fine boots, he has such a kind face that one, you may be sure he will not mind if I go over and speak to him. He will surely permit to me the honour of wearing his wonderful boots, just for a few moments, just long enough to walk around the cantina a few times and get the feel of them on my feet!'

As Pancho spoke these last words, Joe's face had grown red as a blood blister. Now the blister looked about ready to burst. 'Away with you, you impudent rascal!' he bellowed. 'I'll not share no boots a' mine with no thievin' bandit!'

A change came over Pancho Gonzalez. It was as if a different man was standing there beside the table. He seemed to have grown taller, broader. Suddenly he was no longer the humble peasant. The servile mask slipped from his face and behind was something dangerous. It was the face of a cunning man who has put out his bait, waited patiently and now springs his trap. He glowered at Joe. At Sloane. At all three of them.

'A *bandit*!' He had to repeat it several times before he could bring himself to believe it. 'You call me a bandit – me, Pancho Gonzalez?'

He turned to share a piece of his indigation with his *compañeros* at the other table.

'You hear what this stinkin' gringo calls me?' he appealed. 'He dares to call Pancho Gonzalez a *bandido*!'

The six men at the table contrived to look grossly outraged. Some hid their grinning mouths behind their hands. They shook their heads at such an injustice. That a lousy gringo should call Pancho Gonzalez this terrible thing! Pancho turned the heat of his indignation back on the three Americans.

'I am a humble man, gringos,' he told them, 'but I am also proud. And you have hurt my pride. You have hurt me very much. You have wounded my great heart – *mi gran corazón* – which is full of love for all men.'

A second man from his table joined Pancho. It was Pablo, a tall lanky *indito*. Pablo looked very sternly at the three gringos before him, looking at them as might a man who has come to demand satisfaction from the fiends who raped his sister; yet he too held his hat politely in his hands.

'This is a very bad thing you have done,' Pablo said to them reproachfully. 'To call this decent man a bandit. You have hurt him very much I can see. You have hurt his great heart. And now you must show him you are truly sorry for what you have done. You must give to him your wonderful boots.'

Joe's mouth moved up and down but it was a while before he could get the words out. 'Give *him* my boots!' he exploded. His hand slid across the table, reaching for the Colt at his hip. But at the same instant, the three Mexicans standing by the table raised their humbly-held hats and behind each one appeared a heavy calibre pistol. Joe's hand stopped dead as if suddenly nailed to the table.

Pancho's upper lip peeled back from yellow teeth in a broad grin of pleasure. It felt so good to see the foolishness

51

of the three gringos sitting helpless beneath the barrel of his big gun.

While Pancho had been exercising his jaws, Sloane sat with his eyes turned from the Mexican, leaning his tilted head languidly on his arm with the air of someone who has far better things to think about than the unwashed feet of a peasant. Now, he suddenly, grudgingly became interested in what was happening around him. He raised his frosty gaze to the three gun-pointing Mexicans, straightened up and waited to make his move.

'I think I will take those boots now, gringo,' said Pancho with great enjoyment. 'You whose mother is a female dog and your father a goat with no name. And then I will take your money. And then I think maybe I will also take your lives. . .'

The humour of it appealed to Pancho. It made him remember what a helluva clever guy he was. Only someone very smart indeed could have baited the gringo into insulting him as he had done. Now no one would blame him for killing the foolish gringos and taking the boots and money from their bodies. Even the *Federales* understood matters of honour. Pancho threw back his head and laughed a braying jackass laugh.

Then the table hit him. It was a wide table and it also hit Tomas and Pablo. It was the first thing that hit them but it wasn't the last. Right behind the table came Sloane. He followed in a high leap, one foot descending to push Pablo's teeth down his throat, the other kicking the gun from his hand. Sloane landed neatly on both feet and instantly pivoted, his right foot rising in a roundhouse strike that sent Tomas' pistol spinning from a broken hand. Pancho had dropped his gun at the moment of impact with the table. Now he made a grab for it.

'You wanted boots,' Sloane reminded him, closing in, 'try these for size!'

Pancho's hand was an inch short of his pistol when Sloane's boot stamped down on it. Sloane ground his hand into the floor like it was an old cigar butt. Screaming an oath, Pancho tore free his hand. Sloane kicked the gun aside and the same foot leapt up in a flashing arc that caught Pancho under the chin and slammed him against a table. Sloane pursued him with a flying kick, his left boot biting into the pit of Pancho's belly. Pancho crashed over the table then flopped onto the floor, gasping like a fish out of water.

All this happened in less time than it takes most men to blink five times. The men drinking in the Saloon *El Cimarróne* had watched in disbelieving silence as a wild-looking, empty-handed gringo demolished three armed men of dangerous repute. Now all Hell broke loose. Many made a dash for the doors to escape this obvious madman whilst others took refuge under tables. Many more, attracted by the ever-seductive sounds of a fight tried to push in from the plaza outside and watch the fun. The result was a brawling mass of confusion around the doorway. The remaining five friends of Pancho Gonzalez still sitting at their table had been as stunned as everybody else. Probably a lot more. Now they sprang up, sharpened metal glittering in their hands. They charged, overturning chairs in their eagerness to reach this damn gringo and avenge the honour of their comrades. Joe levelled his Walker Colt to blast the charging men. But Billy laid a hand on his arm and winked. Sloane seemed to be doing fine all by himself.

The first Mexican to reach Sloane swung a machete down to cleave his skull. Sloane chopped aside the descending arm with rigid fingers. The man's mouth fell open. Sloane filled it with his boot. The next to reach him favoured a long-bladed knife. Sloane retreated before the slicing blade. Laughing, the man lunged. Sloane's finger's circled his wrist in an iron grip. He squeezed certain nerves. The man shrieked and dropped his blade. Maintaining his grip, Sloane swung the

53

man's body round like a club and cracked his skull against that of the next man. Before they fell, Sloane thrust back his elbow and jabbed it into the eye of Tomas who was trying to aim his gun left-handed. Tomas staggered back, clutching his eye. Sloane helped him on his way with a jarring snap-kick high in the spine. The fourth man was already having second thoughts when he hacked at Sloane's back with his machete. Sloane spun to meet him, catching the blow with a cross-arm block. His left swiped aside the machete whilst his right backfisted the man's groin. The Mexican screamed his agony and doubled up, as if politely bowing to receive the dragon's head punch that spread his nose across his face.

The last man wasn't the impetuous kind. He preferred to keep in the background as he was doing now with a big Starr ·44 tight in his fist. He aimed the long barrel dead in the centre of Sloane's belly and eared back the hammer, finger tightening on the trigger. He was thinking what a big hero he was going to be in the morning, when Billy Wang's flying kick crunched into his kidneys. The shot blasted glasses from a table. The Mexican tried to get off another shot. Billy high-kicked. The pistol flew from his hand and, with it, his trigger finger. A furious flurry of punches and the Mexican hit the floor. Billy sprang over his body and treated Pablo to a fast-moving demonstration of snap-kicks. Sloane watched and liked what he saw. But he didn't get much opportunity to admire Billy's style because Pancho was back on his feet raising his pistol towards him. Sloane's spinning kick tore the gun from his hand. With a snarl of pain, Pancho dipped into his pocket and came up with a knife. He moved towards Sloane, thrusting the knife back and forth before him. It weaved a deadly pattern in the air. Sloane danced around the flashing blade. His foot leapt up and hammered the knife-hand. The knife flew from Pancho's grasp. Mad with pain and fury, Pancho rushed at Sloane, his hands curved like the claws of a beast. Sloane's fist impaled him,

54

stopped him dead in his tracks. A front through-the-heart-kick rattled his rib cage. And then another. The great heart of Pancho Gonzalez shook in its cage. It beat against its bars. It fluttered and failed and grew still as death. Pancho swayed . . . Sloane's high-hooking kick lifted him clear from the ground. His body cannon-balled across the room. Pancho left the saloon without using the door. He crashed through the wooden wall taking a big chunk of it with him into the plaza outside.

Sloane swivelled round, fists raised for more. Then he lowered his arms. There was no one left to hit. Billy had taken care of Pancho's friends that needed taking care of. Most of the saloon's customers had found refuge over by the door where Joe kept them corraled with his pistol. Sloane looked from their open-mouthed faces to the man-sized hole punched through the wall.

'Looks like Pancho's made quite an impression on this place,' he said with a feather of a smile.

'Let's be gettin' the Hell outa here!' Joe urged. The crowd was getting restless and there were more and more of them pushing into the saloon all the time. Pretty soon some hero with a girl to impress was going to start throwing lead in their direction.

Sloane and Billy stepped out through the back-door thoughtfully provided by Pancho. Joe followed, retreating backwards from the crowd.

'Kung Phooey!' he guffawed. 'Why didn't you tell me it was just another name for *fightin' dirty*!'

He kept his pistol handy as they made for the horses. People shrank from the hurrying men, females uttering shrill cries of alarm at the sight of a man brandishing a gun. Angry shouts pursued them from the saloon.

'Think they were El Muerte's men?' Billy asked as they plunged headlong through a gathering crowd.

'No,' said Sloane. 'Small-timers who tried the wrong game with the wrong people.'

By the time they reached their mounts an angry mob was surging in their direction from the saloon. From the other direction a solitary, familiar figure bore down on them with the same determination. It was the dapper American who'd greeted their arrival. Only he didn't look so dapper any more. His hat was tilted, his suit rumpled and he seemed to be having difficulty walking. Sloane would have been prepared to bet good money that his wallet was empty – if he still had one.

His face wrapped itself around a glassy smile he had trouble getting rid of. 'Enjoy your stay, boys?' he asked cordially.

'You bet!' said Billy Wang, swinging into the saddle.

The angry crowd was closer now, much closer. Some of them were chanting '*Maten los gringos* – kill the gringos!'

'Don't talk,' Joe snapped. ' Ride!'

They took his advice. The three of them swept out of town like bats fresh out of Hell. Seconds later the mob, goaded to fury by the sight of their quarry escaping, closed around the dapper American like hungry wolves converging on a lost sheep.

They came across the old man two days later. He was sitting patiently cross-legged by the side of the trail. When they drew closer they saw he was blind, his eyes boiled white like eggs.

'*Buenas tardes, Señores gringos,*' he greeted them. 'I have been awaiting you.'

'Waiting for us?' Joe asked sharply. He glanced around with thoughts of an ambush. He saw no one.

'Are you not the gringos who killed Pancho Gonzalez the famous bandit and crippled his cousin José and many others also?'

Their silence answered his question.

'Yes, I thought it was you,' the old man chuckled. His blindness made his smile seem something intensely personal not meant to be shared with them.

'Good news travels fast,' Sloane observed.

'*Death* travels fast,' said the old man pointedly.

Sloane understood his meaning. 'How fast?' he asked. The trail they were following was cold.

'Faster than you can catch him,' the old man laughed. 'A man may look for death all his life and never find him. And yet when death comes looking for that man, he finds him very fast.'

'We're looking for El Muerte,' said Billy. 'Can you tell us what he looks like?'

Again the old blind man laughed his grating laugh. 'How should I be able to tell you what he looks like, señores? If death were to touch me on the shoulder I would not know him from another, but for the coldness of his touch.'

'I'll know him when I clap eyes on him,' Joe promised. 'And the rest of the murderin' bastards!'

'My people were great princes once,' the old man told them. 'And they will be again. Soon, very soon. We have thrown the French back into the sea from which they came. Now my people grow proud once more. Next it will be the turn of the Americanos. We will throw them out as we have done with the French ones. California will again belong to Mexico. And Texas also.'

Flies crawled over the old man's face but he did not seem to mind.

'The land beyond here is known as *Mictlan*, the land of the dead,' he said, pointing in the direction in which they were headed. 'That is the land of El Muerte!'

'We'll find him,' said Sloane, laying heels to the Morgan. He led the others loping past the old man.

'You will not find El Muerte – but death will find you!' the *viejo* called out after them.

His laughter chased them down the trail.

'Just a crazy old fool!' Billy spoke the thought aloud, his face troubled.

'Maybe so – but I've heard tell some queer tales 'bout these parts,' Joe told his companions. 'The Mexes make out it's full a' evil spirits, make it sound like there's one under every rock in the whole damn place . . . They say there's this one devil grabs ahold a' folks passin' through and eats the meat off a' their bones, picks 'em neat as a wish-bone if you please! Then off he goes an' builds hisself a house with the bones . . . Of course, them Mexes'll believe anythin',' he added lightly.

'You sure make a feller feel at his ease,' said Sloane casting a wary eye over the desert.

It wasn't hard to give weight to Joe's story. Not in the place they found themselves. Not in death's domain. Before them the scorched and thirsty sands stretched to the horizon and beyond like a shimmering sea of bone – the bones of animals and men that had once throbbed with the pulse of life. The desert had snared them all in its trap of thirst and heat. It had snared them and crumpled them, drunk of their blood and shared their flesh with the tearing beaks of buzzards. It chewed them, swallowed them and digested them. Another handful of sand. Another spit in the white ocean.

El Muerte's trail lay ahead of the three men like the desert's own parched thirsty tongue. They followed it right into the grinning jaws of death.

CHAPTER SIX

Pascual gave thanks to El Muerte as he strode towards the cockpit, his tall young son walking proudly at his side. He heaped blessings on the bandit's head. For Pascual was the richest man in the village of Lascara and he owed his wealth all to El Muerte.

Pascual was the village coffin-maker. Before the coming of El Muerte, business had been bad. Pascual had many times thought that nowhere in the whole of Mexico could there be such inconsiderately healthy and long-living people as the citizens of Lascara. He passed the long, idle days seated outside his humble *jacal* waiting for trade that never seemed to come, keeping an interested eye on old shuffling grandmothers, an eager ear open for news of who was sick and who kicked by a stubborn burro and whose wife lay beaten and bleeding in her bed and how so-and-so was going to knife such-and-such when he caught up with that no-good wife-stealing sonovabitch.

Then El Muerte and his bandits had made their camp near the village. And, ever since, Pascual and his son had been as busy as they wished to be. No more could they be seen lounging in the shade of their shack waiting for someone to die. Instead they would be sawing up trees into lengths of six feet – or shavings would be curling endlessly off a rasping plane. Even on Saints' Days, the sound of their insistent hammers could be heard above the tolling of the mission bells. And as fast as he filled his hastily-constructed coffins, Pascual filled his pockets with pesos. For seldom a week passed that someone failed to displease El Muerte – it was so very easy to displease El Muerte – and then screams would shake the village calm, the dogs would bark, widows wail and Pascual would fetch his tools and get straight to work.

So it was not surprising that Pascual offered *mil* blessings to the killer everyone else hated and feared as he walked through the village with his young son, feeling that pleasant gratification men feel when they know they are richer than all those they see around them. Man and boy both had resolute smiles on their faces, their manner suggesting that they were men embarked on a mission that promised enormous satisfaction. As they proceeded towards the cockpit, a ragged collection of barefoot children gathered around them, all noisily expressing their interest in the wicker basket which Pascual carried under his arm with the same pride that a young mother cradles her newborn. For Pascual enjoyed nothing better than a good cockfight and today was Saturday, the day of cockfights. In his basket Pascual carried his new fighting cock, which he had no doubt would be champion by the end of the day. It had better be, he thought. He had paid good money for it, very good money, sending for the bird all the way to Ensenada as only a man of his importance could afford to do. Everyone in the village was anxious to see this marvel in action and none more so than Pascual himself. So far he only had the dealer's word that it could do all the wonderful things claimed for it.

Everyone in the village who could walk and see – and even some who couldn't – were waiting there at the cockpit, the crowd taking the shape of the circular arena. In grander days the arena had been the scene of many a *corrida*. Now the villagers had to content themselves with fighting cocks instead of bulls. Pascual and his son walked straight to the centre of the arena where a knot of men were standing waiting. With satisfaction, Pascual noted that José the *pulque*-vendor, owner of Lobo, the reigning champion, lacked his usual bright air of confidence.

After a brief exchange of greetings, Pascual kneeled and

opened his basket. The circle of onlookers tightened, men craning their necks to get a better look at this bird which had cost enough money to feed every mouth in the village for days. Pascual lifted the bird from the basket and held it high for all to see. The crowd murmured its approval. The cock, which Pascual had hopefully named Vampiro, was a mean-looking bird. It was smaller than its opponent, Lobo, but looked more lively and alert. Its bright beady eyes glared evilly from side to side, suspicious of all it could see. It irritably nipped a piece of Pascual's hand between the sharp points of its beak. Pascual took this as a good omen and shrugged aside the pain.

'Well, José,' he demanded of the *pulque*-vendor, 'do you still think your old chicken can beat my Vampiro – or do you wish to call off our bet?' He knew, of course, that the *pulque*-vendor could not back out without losing face in the eyes of the other villagers and this he would never do.

'It is as we said – fifty pesos to the winner,' José affirmed.

'*Muy bien*,' Pascual nodded and held the bird stiff-legged so that Juan could tie the wicked, glinting spurs to its feet.

When both owners had completed their preparations, they held the two birds close together – close enough to taunt but not to bite. Their hackles rose at the sight and smell of one another. Their heads jerked back and forth as they strained to peck at each other's eyes. Holding the birds at arm's length, Pascual and José stepped back until about seven feet separated the two fighters. The men waited for Manolo the basket-weaver to give his signal. Manolo let flutter his handkerchief to the ground and the waiting men released their birds.

The cocks flew straight at each other. They met in mid-air, flapping desperately, each trying to climb higher than the other. Their scrawny yellow legs pumped a crazy dance, blurs of yellow and slashing silver. Beaks clamped on wings and the two birds became a red fluttering ball spinning and spinning. Feathers splashed the air. The two cocks tore themselves apart and fell awkwardly to the ground. Both landed running. They clashed again, became furiously embroiled. Dust swirled around them in feather-flecked clouds.

'At him, Lobo!' yelled José the *pulque*-vendor. 'Cut him to pieces!'

'Go, Vampiro, go! Tear out his goddam eyes!' screamed Pascual, pounding the air with his fist.

These sentiments were hotly taken up by each of the crowd according to preference.

The two birds leapt apart, both speckled with blood from a dozen small bites and tears. They circled each other, wary as boxers in a ring. Lobo was bigger, but Vampiro had the advantage of speed. Again they threw themselves at each other, pecking and slashing. Lobo managed to get above Vampiro. He snapped his beak tight on Vampiro's comb, the cracked yellow beak becoming wet and red. His legs thrashed, spike-tipped feet hunting flesh to carve. It looked like the end for Vampiro. Pascual groaned. He thought of the money wasted, the prestige lost. His sleeve mopped at his dripping forehead. He dared not raise his eyes from the battling cocks in case they met the taunting gaze of the *pulque*-vendor.

But Vampiro was not yet finished. He twisted and wheeled to break free of the biting pain of Lobo's beak. Lobo held on through all the evasions, beak clamped determinedly onto comb. Vampiro leapt up. The two birds whirled fluttering into the air. Then Vampiro's stabbing spur found a soft place. Lobo squawked, releasing his hold. He fell twisting to the reddened soil. Vampiro plunged down after him, one spur ramming into an eye. Lobo's thrashing spasm of pain weakened slowly into twitching death. Vampiro went on pecking at the savaged body until it lay completely still. Then he strutted back and forth beside the body, lustily proclaiming his victory.

Pascual raised his champion in firm but adoring hands.

He hugged the bird then handed him to Juan to care for his wounds. He felt like crowing aloud himself. He looked around, proud and smiling. People shouted their congratulations. He received them with the gracious tolerance of a man who had never for an instant doubted that his bird would triumph. He looked over at the *pulque*-vendor. José was gathering up the remains of the ex-champion, lifting the body reverently as he would the corpse of his own son. They would be eating chicken soup tonight in the *jacal* of the *pulque*-vendor, he thought with a smile. But nobody would enjoy it much.

Pascual tugged contentedly at his greying moustachios. He had come as a rich man and he would leave the cockpit richer still. The thought made him so happy that he almost did not notice the horsemen until they were all around him.

The villagers stumbled back before the shoving intrusion of the snorting stamping horses and their loud-voiced riders. They humbled their suddenly hatless heads beneath the mocking grins in the faces of the bandits. In silence they suffered the scornful abuse thrown at them like stones. The few that dared raise their heads had eyes only for the man riding the blackest of black horses, a tall, spectral figure rearing high and straight from a silver-worked saddle. The tall man on the black horse swung his eyes across the faces of the villagers like a lash.

'Is there a maker of coffins here?' El Muerte demanded. 'One who calls himself Pascual?' There was a caress in his voice, a purring caress that almost hid the contemptuous scorn.

'I am he, señor . . .' Pascal stepped forward almost eagerly, an arm half-raised for recognition. In his head he was already rubbing his palms. More dead, he thought. More dead, more coffins, more *pesos*.

El Muerte waved a wagon forward. The grinning driver reined in alongside Pascual, the horses churning dust. Pascual stared at the wagon. In the back lay a coffin. He recognised it without hesitation as one of his own.

El Muerte made an impatient gesture, flicking his wrist towards the driver of the wagon. Rings sparkled on his fingers. Boots scraped across wagon-boards, spurs jangling. Strong hands pushed the coffin and heaved it to the ground. The coffin rolled, the lid bursting open. A body tumbled out at Pascual's feet. With difficulty he recognised the mutilated face. It belonged to a bandit who had spoken disrespectfully of El Muerte when drunk in the cantina one night.

'You made this coffin?' El Muerte asked.

'Yes, señor,' Pascal admitted with uncertain pride. 'With the help of my son, Juan.' He rested a hand on the boy's shoulder. He wanted El Muerte to see what a strong helpful son he had.

El Muerte climbed slowly down from the black horse. He walked purposefully towards the coffin and Pascual, six and a half feet of midnight moving across the arena in the afternoon sun. His body made music as he moved. A tiny golden bell tinkled sweetly from one ear. Gold coins sewn onto his black jacket and black conchoed trousers jingled and chattered. His holsters creaked beneath the weight of heavy guns. But louder than all of these was the regular shivering rattle of his spurs, jumping and jangling at every step. The spurs rose from the back of his stack-heeled boots like the quivering sting of a scorpion. They were silver these spurs and long, each one shaped like a scythe. The eyes of all the villagers were on the spurs as El Muerte approached Pascual. For they knew what these spurs could do. And what they had done.

El Muerte nudged the shattered coffin with the square toe of his boot. His eyes filled Pascual's horizon.

'This is not a good coffin,' said El Muerte in a voice like a judge passing sentence. 'This is a very bad coffin. I would not bury a dog in a coffin such as this. Not even a dog such as him!' As he spoke the last words, his voice rising in anger, El Muerte kicked the body of the dead bandit.

Something whimpered in the pit of Pascual's stomach. He wished he could throw himself down and dig a hole in the dust and disappear inside it. Or that he might suddenly wake up and find himself safe and wealthy at the start of another profitable day with his naked thigh pressed up against the plump pillow-like buttocks of Maria the village whore. None of these things happened. Instead he found himself still uncomfortably at the centre of the arena, face to face with death.

In twenty years as a coffin-maker, Pascual had seen and handled death in many forms – bodies blackened by scorpion stings, baked by the sun, shattered by cannon-balls, mangled by cart-wheels. All of these and worse he had put to bed in their final resting place. But never had he seen anything as terrible as this living death which glared at him with furious narrow-slitted eyes – eyes that scorched into his and gave his soul a foretaste of Hell.

'The dead must be honoured,' said El Muerte, his voice slow-burning in anger. 'And your coffins are not fit for the dead!'

The anger of El Muerte flared up like coal-oil on a fire. He kicked at the ruined coffin. He kicked at it and stamped on it – smashing apart the flimsy boards. His anger was a fearful thing to see. Old black-shawled women whose ancient eyes had seen everything crossed themselves at the sight. The faces of hardened men grew pale and lesser men sweated and trembled as if struggling with a fever.

As Pascual was doing now.

El Muerte stood above the splintered fragments of the coffin, his chest heaving. He seemed to be trying to control the madness that inflamed his brain. He glared at the coffin-maker trembling before him and then at his son. The smouldering eyes fell upon the cock Juan held in palsied hands.

'This bird . . . he is yours?' El Muerte asked the coffin-maker.

'Yes, señor . . .'

'You like to watch him fight with other birds?'

'Oh, yes, señor!' Pascual assured him, anxious to please. 'It is my whole life.'

El Muerte smiled the smile of a man who had suddenly found the solution to a nagging problem. 'Then let it be your death,' he said. 'So you will know how it is to die in the dirt to please other men like you – men with no respect for Death!'

Ignoring the faint wail of despair that sprung from Pascual's bloodless lips, El Muerte called out to his men who were watching from their horses with silent, slack-mouthed amusement: 'Give them weapons that they may fight like men and not like birds!'

A machete was tossed to Pascual. A sword clattered at Juan's feet. Another bandit nudged his horse forward and snatched Vampiro squawking from Juan's hands. Whooping, he spun the bird in a flapping circle round his head – then tossed it like a cabbage into the ranks of villagers. Others rode their horses stiff-legged against the crowd, forcing the villagers to retreat further back.

'Pick up your weapons,' El Muerte ordered the trembling man and boy.

Father and son looked at one another for a moment that seemed endless. Then they stooped and lifted the weapons. They weighed the unfamiliar blades in their hands, testing their balance.

'Now let's see if you crow as loudly as your birds . . .' said El Muerte, his smile carnivorous.

The three men were a triangle inside the larger circle of the cockpit. Juan attacked first, his sword raised high to slash at the bandit's head. El Muerte side-stepped and sent the boy sprawling with a kick in the pants that raised a laugh from his men. Now Pascual tried his luck. He ran forward and lashed out with the machete. El Muerte dodged the blow then sprang up, leaping high in the air, lashing out with his boot at the side of Pascual's head. Pascual's hand flew to his ear and found only blood. His ear lay in the dust.

El Muerte stood with his hands on his hips and laughed a cavernous laugh. With a shriek of anger, Juan launched himself at the laughing bandit. He thrust with his sword and missed. He swiped in a broader arc – and missed again. The third time, El Muerte's foot leapt up. Spurs slashed through skin and muscle, scraped on bone. Juan howled. The sword dropped from pain-flexed fingers. The boy clutched his arm, his white shirt becoming scarlet.

El Muerte's men cheered as if they were applauding a skilful pass by a great toreador at the *Plaza de Toros* in Mexico City. The bandit chief had no time to acknowledge his men's appreciation and take a bow because Pascual was upon him, hacking with the machete like a madman, his face flushed with hate and fear and blood from his pumping wound. El Muerte danced from the hissing blade, coins and spurs jangling a mocking tune. Amused, he watched the older man make himself breathless in vain. Then the bandit snapped out a kick. The machete sprang from Pascual's grasp. Through tears of pain Pascual watched the blood gush from his wrist. El Muerte's vaulting cry of pleasure alerted him to the next kick. He stumbled backwards, jerking his head away from the boot rushing at his face. The boot caught him under the chin, the silver spurs slicing through his neck and slitting his jugular. Pascual collapsed in the dust by Lobo's body. Somehow, he managed to struggle up onto his knees. Like a very weary man who can hardly keep his eyes open, Pascual watched his veins empty into the dust, feeding the thirsty sand. It took much less time than he expected for his veins to run dry. He toppled forward onto the crimson sand and lay still, dead as Lobo.

He was the lucky one.

Juan retreated from El Muerte's advance in a tearful panic. There was nowhere he could run to. He was trapped inside a solid circle of horseflesh and steel. With death for company. Without any hope, he ran and snatched the sword from where it had fallen. Holding it awkwardly in his left hand, he turned to face his father's killer. El Muerte advanced steadily towards him. There was no doubt in his face as to what the outcome of this duel would be.

Juan attacked. It was a clumsy attack. He ran at El Muerte and slashed with the sword. El Muerte was no longer where he had been. The sword whistled over his head. He danced out of range. Juan made to follow – then tripped over the body of the dead bandit. He pitched to the ground.

El Muerte looked down at him with disappointment, with amused pity. The boy struggled up, using the sword as a support. Through a veil of blood and sweat he saw El Muerte standing there waiting for him, smiling his contempt. Juan screamed his hatred at the bandit. He ran at him, the sword flashing wildly ... This time El Muerte did not side-step. He threw himself into the air and kicked out. The raking spur slashed a red line up one side of Juan's face, neatly cutting through his left eye.

Juan pitched into the dust, hands to his face, and screamed.

El Muerte strode over to the writhing boy. 'Take him to the mission,' he called out so that all the villagers could hear. 'Let the old women who call themselves priests see to him!'

El Muerte walked from the boy towards his horse. On the way something caught his eye. He stooped and picked it from the dust. Then he approached the villagers, searching amongst their empty-eyed faces. He found what he was looking for – a young girl who would have been pretty had it not been for the bitterness which veiled her youth.

'For you, Carmen,' he smiled, pressing something cold and moist into her hand. 'The ear of the bull should always go to the prettiest girl in the crowd.'

The bandits grinned like monkeys. There was not one amongst them who had not sunk his flesh into the flesh of Carmen many times. Carmen looked at Pascual's bleeding ear in her hand, stared at it as if it were a scorpion nestling on her palm. Yet she did not throw it down. A life with shame was better than no life at all. Her hand closed tight around the ear.

'*Gracias*, señor,' she said and curtsied. Her lips even succeeded in forming a smile of thanks.

'*De nada*, señorita,' the bandit smiled, clicking his heels and bowing with mocking courtesy.

El Muerte mounted his black horse and galloped from the arena, scattering villagers. His men followed in a pack close behind, yipping and yeying.

Later, José the *pulque*-vendor took home his new champion fighting cock, feeling considerably more than fifty pesos wealthier and musing that the ways of men and God were strange but not without their small rewards.

'Jesus, it's hot 'nough to sweat the Devil's tail,' Joe Hardy told himself, loud enough for Sloane and Billy Wang to hear.

Their horses were hoofing through an endless rolling sea of baking sand, and blistering heat poured down onto their heads like the sun had a personal grudge against them. They seemed to be taking a long time getting nowhere. Except that the tracks of El Muerte's gang still stretched ahead like a welcoming red carpet leading them ever deeper into the land of death.

'Well, now, here I am ridin' through somewheres what's hotter'n Hell to me certain death,' Joe mused, 'in comp'ny with a heathen Chinee an' a feller that looks like he's just missed his own funeral – and not a word a' decent conversation between the two of 'em! If that ain't a sign I've gone an' lost what little good sense the Lord saw fit to gi'me, I don't know what is ...'

Sloane and Billy weren't the only company Joe had. Above, patient buzzards followed their slow progress, wheeling over their heads in wide lazy circles. Joe eyed them defiantly.

'Stick around as long as you want, ya squawkin' devils,' he told the buzzards, 'but you'll wait till this hell freezes over afore you gets a free meal outta Joe Hardy!'

Joe swung round on his two human companions.

'Promise me one thing, boys – that if I gets called to me maker, you'll give me a grave to rest me bones in ... with a marker so folks'll know that patch a' dirt's just a mite different from all the rest.'

'You keep airin' that mouth of yours the way you been doin' and we won't wait till you're dead before burying you,' Sloane told him.

It was Sloane who first saw the tepee. A tepee where no tepee ought to be. It stood in the middle of nowhere surrounded by nothing. Nothing alive that is. They rode towards it. It wasn't like any tepee any of them had ever seen before. The skin covering the frame was fresh-scraped rawhide with no Indian markings. There was a chair outside the tepee. The legs of the chair were human shin-bones. A short distance from the tepee rose a great heap of bones of all shapes and sizes. And beside that was a smaller mound of skulls, mostly human. There was smoke curling from the smoke-hole of the tepee.

The three men sat on their restlessly shifting horses looking at the heap of bones and the chair with the human legs and the pile of skulls and all three thought about Joe's story of the bone devil the Mexicans believed in, the evil spirit that grabbed hold of passing strangers and stripped the flesh from their bones.

'Come on in – coffee's on the boil!' a cordial voice invited from within the tepee.

'I'm thinkin' it's time to be movin' on,' said Joe with sudden urgency.

Without replying, Sloane swung down off his horse and slowly approached the tepee. He drew back the flap and peered inside. He was greeted by a smell of coffee and a dazzling white smile in a dark face. The face belonged to a tall negro with regular clean-cut features. He looked about thirty-five and there was nothing unusual about him as far as Sloane could see. Except that he only had hair on one side of his head. One side there was a close-curling crop of deep brown hair streaked with gray. The other side was smooth as an egg.

'Hi, there!' the negro welcomed. 'Ain't yo' friends comin' in for coffee?'

Sloane turned back to his companions and beckoned them forward with a jerk of his head. Reassured to see that Sloane still had meat on his bones and was not already a skeleton, Joe and Billy joined him.

'Dred Jefferson's the name,' the negro told them and cheerfully rubbed palms with the three of them.

They sat inside Dred's tepee and drank his coffee. There were more skulls inside the tepee, neat little piles of them all gleaming and brightly polished. Each time Joe's eyes fell on them he pulled a face, wrinkling up his nose like he was downwind of a mule-skinner. He peered suspiciously into the dark and steamy depths of his cup for tell-tale signs of a Mickey Finn. He didn't want to wake up later and find himself looking down from atop one of those neat little piles.

'Guess you folks is wonderin' what I's doin' with all them bones all over, huh?' Dred asked good-humouredly.

'It had kinda crossed our minds,' Sloane admitted.

Dred chuckled richly. 'I'm in the bone-pickin' business,' he told them. 'Done found me some people'll take all the bones I kin find. I picks the bones an' they makes 'em into fert'liser to put on the ground.'

Billy reached out and plucked one of the skulls from a pile. He balanced it on his palm, peering into the sightless sockets. 'I never knew they made fertiliser out of people,' he said conversationally.

Dred's laughter boomed melodiously around the tepee. 'Don't reckon they does neither,' he said. 'But you knows what they says – "Ashes to ashes, dust to dust!"' Turning, he fondly patted the top skull of a pile at his side.

'I got me a side-line,' he revealed. 'There ain't much profit in the fert'liser bus'ness no more. But there's a feller back east pays fat money for skulls like these 'uns here. A dollar fifty for an Injun skull, two fifty for a white man's. Three dollars for somethin' real fine. He sells 'em again for a whole lot more money ... I guess to folks lookin' for somethin' cosy to stick on their mantel-shelves. If'n it's a Injun skull he tells how the Injun done got hisself killed raidin' a wagon train. With a white man's skull he makes out the feller was some mighty fine hero died savin' some chilluns from the Apaches!'

'How 'bout a nigger's skull?' Joe asked huffily. 'How much d'you get for that?'

Dred flashed his teeth at Joe. 'We's all white folks un'neath, mister,' he said without offence. He leaned over and rapped his big knuckles vigorously on the dome of a skull.

'*Bone*-white!' he laughed.

'I still reckon it's a dirty business,' said Joe. 'Sellin' the skulls outta the heads a' decent folk like they was just so many cabbages in a heap.'

The negro looked pained. His smile retreated. 'Shoot, it's as honest a livin' as any,' he said defensively. 'Just tidyin' up other folks' mess is all. No harm in that. Why, I guess if I wasn't doin' it, it'd be somebody else, sho' 'nough.'

'Man's gotta make a living,' Sloane pointed out generously.

'When we saw your tepee, we figured you for a bone-devil,' said Billy.

'*A bone-devil*,' Dred repeated with slow delight. He liked the name and he showed his approval with a deep sonorous chuckle.

'Yeah, I guess that's what I am, f'sure – a bone-devil!' He went on chuckling, right up until Sloane said:

'We're looking for El Muerte. Any idea where we might find him?'

'El Muerte!' The name punched Dred's smile right off his face. He stared wide-eyed at Sloane, then shook his head slowly from side to side. 'You sure don't wanna mess none with him,' he said.

'We aim to mess with him plenty,' Joe assured him.

Dred was silent for a moment, his massive shoulders hunched over his dipped and brooding head.

'All I can tell you's 'bout El Muerte,' he said finally, 'is he usually hangs around a village near here by the name of Lascara. But you'd be crazy to go anywhere near there. He don't like strangers no better'n he likes nobody else. Only good thing 'bout him is he's sure good for bus'ness. Pickin's been real fine since he done showed up . . .' Dred nodded, his smile creeping back. 'Yah, real fine.'

The faces of the other men hardened against him.

'I think business is gonna take a turn for the worse,' said Sloane.

'Uh-uh, no way!' the bone-devil grinned. 'If you three is ridin' out lookin' for El Muerte, I got me a feelin' bus'ness is gonna get a whole lot *better*!'

'Let's be on our way,' said Joe, his voice strained harsh. He stood up to leave. The other two followed.

Billy hesitated. 'There's something I just gotta ask you,' he said to Dred.

Dred clapped a big brown hand over the bald side of his skull. 'You bin wonderin' 'bout my hair, ain't you?' he said knowingly.

Billy nodded.

'Shoot, that's nothin',' Dred laughed. ''Fore I come down this way, I was in the Cavalry with the boys in blue. One time we was out on a patrol when a pack of Cheyenne hit us. Whole patrol done got themselves wiped out. There was just me left and I was pretty wiped out myself, let me tell you. Then along comes a Cheyenne an' starts to gi'me this here Injun haircut. I told him straight I didn't want no haircut offa him but he just wasn't payin' me no heed at all. Then up comes this big ole chief an' he done took one look at me an' he says – "Hey, leave that boy be – can't you see he's brother to the buff'lo spirit?" Man, there wasn't nothin' them Injuns wouldn't do for me after that!'

Dred followed the three men to their horses, his tall lean body moving with catlike grace. Sloane saw the negro looking at him in a sly-smiling way and he wondered what he had that Dred wanted. Then he knew. His head.

'That's some fine piece of goods you got there 'tween your shoulders, Missuh Sloane,' said Dred admiringly. 'Yessir, that's sho' 'nough a three dollar special. Hope it don't get messed up too bad when you meets up with that El Muerte.'

Sloane looked down at the negro from the saddle. His thin mouth tightened into a suspicion of a smile. 'I'll ask 'em to shoot low,' he said.

CHAPTER SEVEN

The soil grew red on the trail to Lascara – like a great drop of blood had splashed down out of the sky and given a bit of life back to the death-lands. Clumps of ocotillo began to eat greenly into the desert, timidly at first then voraciously. Lofty *cadrons* sprang up, reaching for heaven with their many-fingered arms. Cirio trees bowed their withered tapering heads in respect to the three men riding past. They were riding towards the twin towers of the mission which rose blackly against a gaudy sky. As they rode nearer they could see the village beyond the mission, an impoverished collection of shacks and a few small houses of adobe. El Muerte had chosen his name well, Sloane decided. The village looked like it had died a long time ago.

People shouted when they saw the three men riding in out of the wavering heat. They shouted in fear and ran like they had just seen a whole regiment of enemy infantry advancing on them with fixed bayonets. They took refuge inside the sturdy mission walls. By the time Sloane and his two trail companions reached the mission there wasn't a soul to be seen.

Then one of the mission doors creaked open and a broad heavy-set man appeared. He hurried towards them, his black robe flopping to and fro above his sandalled feet. Gravely, he positioned himself in the path of the three strangers.

'I do not bid you welcome, señores,' said the priest, 'for you have the misfortune to find yourselves in the village of Lascara.'

'Then we're in the right place,' said Sloane.

The priest looked at Sloane with pity, pity for this hard-faced Americano who did not know his danger, pity for the tormented people of Lascara, pity for himself.

'No, señor,' he shook his head, 'you are mistaken. Lascara has not been the right place for many years. Now you must return – go back to where you have come from.'

Joe addressed the priest in a tone of enormous patience. 'Padre, we've been travellin' for days through some a' the hottest country this side a' Hell – an' now you're tellin' us to turn ourselves right round an' go all the way back again without doin' what we came for ... There's no sense in that at all!'

The priest seemed tortured by indecision. He looked from face to face searchingly. Finally, his expression mellowed. 'Forgive me, señores,' he said repentently. 'It is not my wish to appear discourteous. I am Father Francesco and this which you see before you is the mission of San Pietro. Will you not join me inside for a glass of *limon* or wine if you prefer ... But then you must go,' he added more firmly.

'Seems to me you're mighty anxious to get rid of us,' said Sloane.

Father Francesco nodded. 'There is much danger for you here,' he said. 'Terrible danger.'

They hitched their horses and followed the priest into the mission. Father Francesco was a big man, big enough to have been a *vaquero* or even a prize-fighter. But the eyes set in his broad strong face were those of a priest – warm, compassionate and contemplative. They were also troubled eyes, for Father Francesco did not always find it easy to be both a man of strength and a priest. There were times when he was plagued by the thought that he might be better able to help his people with the strength of his big body than with the strength of his faith. Such times had become disturbingly numerous lately.

He led the three Americans through his church. Several shawled women and an aged man were kneeling in prayer,

76

their heads bowed towards the altar with its many flickering candles. Pine needles were strewn on the floor. They made the church smell cool and good after the airless heat of the desert. The four men emerged into an open courtyard. There were vines in the courtyard. And white roses and flowering trees of various kinds. There were also people in the courtyard. People that looked at the strangers with frightened eyes – those of them who were fortunate enough to have eyes to look. For some were blind, their empty eye-sockets masked by patches. Others were horribly mutilated, their noses or lips cut from their faces. Some lacked a limb – an arm or a leg or both.

A scurrying movement down low made Sloane lower his eyes. Two legless men were scuttling along like crabs, fleeing from his gaze behind the legs of the others. Their torsos were supported on small trolleys with squeaking wheels and they pushed themselves forward with their hands. The men and women in the courtyard looked like the civilian casualties of a long, cruel war.

'What happened to these people?' Sloane asked the priest.

Father Francesco knew only too well the suffering faces of his flock. Many a night they crept into his dreams – crept and crawled and hopped on crutches. He did not turn to look at them now.

'*Pobrecitos*,' he murmured. 'Death has done these things to them. They have felt the pain of his bite but not its release. We call them the Unfortunate Ones.'

Shaking his head, Father Francesco led them to the room where he spent most of his time when he was not in prayer or tending to his flowers or his flock. It was a small cool room, sparsely furnished with a cupboard, a table, chairs and some books. There was a plaster madonna praying in an alcove and a gilt-framed picture of a fierce Christ on one wall. A smell of incense hung sweetly about the room. A youth sat dully on one of the chairs, staring one-eyed into space whilst another priest, younger than Father Francesco, bandaged his injured eye. An old woman, black-robed and cowled, watched the bandaging with grieving attention, her hands pressed tight together.

Father Francesco and the three Americans waited by the doorway for the younger priest to complete his work.

'I will come and see you later, Juan,' the priest promised the boy when he was through, laying a comforting hand on his shoulder. The priest nodded to the old woman. She helped Juan from the chair and led the boy by one arm past the newcomers. Sloane looked at the boy as he passed. The boy seemed numb from some kind of shock. His free arm dangled uselessly at his side

'It is a dreadful thing to see one so young lose the sight of his eye,' said Father Francesco sympathetically when the old woman and the boy were gone. Turning, he raised his hand towards the younger priest who had stepped forward, eyeing the strangers with unveiled curiosity.

'This is Father Josef,' he told them, 'my companion in the work of the mission.'

Father Josef greeted each of the travellers in turn, grasping their hands firmly in his own. He was a small man, barely taller than five feet. His size, together with the flowing monk's habit, made him appear delicate – yet the robes hid a lean sinewy body capable of quick confident movement. His brown straight hair was cut in a fringe which nearly touched the dark smudges of his eyebrows and a neat half-moon beard disguised a weakish chin. There was nothing weak about the eyes though. Whereas the eyes of Father Francesco were inward-turned and meditative, those of Father Josef peered brightly out at the world with a piercing and demanding gaze. Something in the dark bright eyes implied that most of what they saw dissatisfied the young priest and that here was a man who longed to do something to lessen his dissatisfaction.

The Americans accepted an invitation to make themselves comfortable and stretched out in chairs around the room. They persuaded Father Francesco to pour out glasses, not of *limon* but of the sombre sweet *vino* made from the grapes of the mission vineyard.

'That boy – and those people out there – is that El Muerte's work?' Sloane asked when he had approved the wine.

Father Francesco glanced quickly over at Sloane, a suggestion of alarm springing into his eyes. 'You know of El Muerte?' he asked.

Joe cut himself into the conversation with a chuckle. 'Padre, seems to me there's two kinds a' people round here,' he said. 'Them's as have heard of El Muerte an' them he's up an' killed.'

Father Francesco leaned forward in his chair, bowing his head over clasped hands. He looked suddenly older, greyer.

'The boy that you saw – El Muerte did this terrible thing to him only yesterday. At the same time he killed the boy's father – Pascual the coffin-maker.' The priest sighed wearily. 'Now we have no coffin in which to bury the coffin-maker decently.'

'How long's this been goin' on?' Sloane asked.

'For too long,' said Father Josef sharply. 'Far too long.'

Father Francesco gave the younger priest a look of gentle rebuff before answering Sloane's question. 'For nearly two years now,' he said, 'El Muerte has plagued Lascara. There is not a family in the village who does not mourn a father or a son killed by the bandit. Or a daughter ravished by him and his band of killers.'

'He is a terrible man,' said Father Josef. 'A demon.'

'Terrible, yes,' agreed the older priest, 'but no demon. He is a man like other men except in his cruelty which is like that of the jaguar. I knew him when he was younger. Then he went by the name of Arrabal and he was an honest man.

79

He went away to sea – they say he journeyed to many distant lands. Only when he returned did he call himself El Muerte and begin his ways of cruelty and blood.'

'Why hasn't the government helped your village?' Billy asked. 'They could have sent in troops to wipe out El Muerte.'

Father Josef uttered a sharp scornful laugh. 'There are many in Mexico who consider El Muerte to be a hero because he kills gringos – *perdóneme*, señores,' he added apologetically. 'So the *politicos* do nothing. What does it matter to them if El Muerte kills a few peasants when it pleases him – as long as he boasts that he will take California from the Americanos and give it back to Mexico.'

'If I was livin' in a place where El Muerte was massacreein' everybody in sight, I reckon I'd be hightailin' it outta there pretty snappy,' said Joe.

'So it would be in most villages, señor,' Father Josef agreed, nodding vigorously. 'But in Lascara the people accept these deaths, these tortures as a punishment from Heaven – the will of God. They think it is part of the curse...'

The priest saw that he held the attention of the three visitors.

'Yes, señores, there is a curse on the village of Lascara. It was not always a place of death and fear. Once it was a happy village, a place of pilgrimage famous throughout all Mexico for the piety of its people. Pilgrims came from all over to this very mission in which we are sitting. They came to kneel and do penance for their sins before the Holy Skull...'

As he spoke of the skull, the young priest's eyes gleamed still more brightly and his whole face was lit up with pious ecstasy – as if he himself were kneeling before the sacred object.

'I have never seen this skull, señores,' he said, 'but I have heard speak of its beauty many times. It is not the skull from the head of a man but was carved from crystal by the hands of great artists. It is faultless in its perfection – exquisite! And the colour of the skull is red – for in its crystal veins are a few precious drops of the *sangre del Cristo* – the blood of Christ torn from his brow by the crown of thorns!'

There was silence in the room for a moment as Father Josef paused to let the significance of his words sink in. Joe's gaze crept up the wall and met the fierce eyes of the Christ hanging there. He stared at the picture.

'Yes,' said Father Josef, his dark eyes sparkling, 'the blood of the Son of God ... Our books tell us the skull was found in the Holy Land by monks of our order. They took it to Spain. From there it was brought to Mexico by the monks who founded this mission.'

'What happened to the skull?' Billy asked.

The face of the young priest lost its ecstasy. His expression grew bitter. 'One Sunday as the pilgrims were arriving for Mass, armed men attacked the mission. They killed the pilgrims – women, children, everybody! They spared no one, not even the priests. The name of him who led those killers is Don Luis Fernando de Silviera. *He* took the skull ... Since that day there has been nothing but misfortune and sadness in the village of Lascara. And so it will be until the skull is returned to the mission.'

His tale completed, Father Josef sat back in his chair and looked at the three Americans.

'Quite a story,' Sloane remarked.

'Imagine that,' Joe marvelled, 'blood from the veins of our Lord – right here in this little place!' His expression was one of awe.

'Not all men are convinced that the blood is that of our Christ. Or that the skull is an object of good,' said Father Francesco quietly. 'I regret that Father Josef and I have our differences of opinion on this matter.'

Father Josef looked heatedly at the older priest. For a moment it appeared that he might speak to him in anger. But then he caught the rebellious impulse and repressed it. Instead, he turned back to the Americans.

'You have come a long way?' he asked.

Sloane told him how far they'd come. The priest grew thoughtful.

'Men would not travel so far without a good reason,' he observed.

'I got a good reason,' said Sloane.

'May I inquire what is the nature of your reason?'

'I'm gonna kill El Muerte,' said Sloane, matter-of-factly.

Father Francesco looked despairingly at the hard-faced American with the cold eyes. Suddenly he realised Sloane looked familiar to him. There was a bleakness in his eyes the priest had seen before. He'd seen it in the eyes of El Muerte. It was the look of a hardened killer.

'I should never have brought you in here,' he said dejectedly to the three men. 'I must insist that you leave when you have finished your wine – and that you do not return.'

Father Josef led Sloane and his companions back to their horses.

'Father Francesco would not approve of what I say,' he told them with the unease of a conspirator, 'but I wish you luck in your mission. To kill a devil such as El Muerte must be God's work I am sure ... In the wine cellars beneath the mission are many barrels of gunpowder. I have often thought that with the help of some good men I could take the gunpowder and rid our people of this evil. With only one barrel –' He broke off abruptly, screwing up his face. He shrugged. 'Perhaps Father Francesco is right,' he continued, 'what kind of talk is this for a priest of God?'

'Tell me more about that gunpowder,' said Sloane as they emerged into the sunlight outside the church.

'For a few months the mission was occupied as a garrison

82

by the French. When they retreated the powder was left behind and they never returned. We have never spoken of it to anyone for fear that El Muerte might get to hear about it. Can you imagine what devilry that bandit could commit with so much gunpowder? *Quien sabe?* It is too terrible even to think of!'

The small priest watched the Americans mount their horses. They looked tall and confident in the saddle. The sight gave him hope. If El Muerte could be destroyed these men might be able to do it.

'I think perhaps you can rid us of this evil one, señores,' he said. 'Yes, I am sure of it. I feel that God smiles on you.'

Sloane seemed amused but said nothing.

'Don't you worry none, padre,' said Joe. 'When we get through with him, El Muerte's gonna wish he really was dead!'

'I hope it will be so,' said the priest.

'Is there a *cantina* in the village?' Sloane asked.

'Only one,' said Father Francesco. '*El Gato Negro* ... a place of bad repute but I am told their food is good.'

'Obliged,' said Sloane. He touched his hat and put heels to the Morgan.

The priest watched the three men raising dust as they headed for the village. 'Good fortune in your hunting, señores!' he cried, waving. '*Vayan con Dios!*'

The three men rode amongst the shanties of the village pursued by lean, barking dogs. The smell of the place led them to *El Gato Negro*. They reined in alongside the *cantina*.

The small saloon was bursting with laughter and eager conversation. When the three Americans entered, the place became silent as the grave. Dark-faced *peons* looked up from the *pulque*, staring at the intruders with eyes of beaten dogs. The *cantina* was well-known for the excellence of its *tamales*. There wasn't an empty seat in the room and none of the silent hostile men looked like they were going to break a leg to make room for the intruding gringos.

'Anybody here know where we can find El Muerte?' Joe called out suddenly, rupturing the silence.

There was a scuffling rush for the door. Within a minute the three Americans had the whole place to themselves.

They fed their hunger on *tacos* and *tamales*.

Later, they rode out of the small village, their faces set hard and determined. They'd come a long way after El Muerte and now they were about to meet up with him, face to face. Even Joe was silent, his thoughts on the fight ahead. His fingers curled tight round Old Henry.

Soon the village had faded behind them like a mirage. The sun was waiting for them, hot and blinding as ever – and so were their old friends the buzzards. This time the buzzards were in luck. Joe had a cigar clamped between his teeth but it could have been a stick of dynamite the way his head blew apart when the bullet struck.

CHAPTER EIGHT

'Down!' Sloane yelled.

He touched dust before Joe's body. He'd leapt from the Morgan's back the instant the crisp thunderclap of the rifle-shot burst on his ears. He took cover behind his nerve-rattled horse, wrapping his hand in the reins. Billy joined him, crouching.

'Here, hold this,' Sloane snapped, tossing the reins to Billy. Stooping, he dragged the Henry rifle from Joe's twitching fingers. Kung Fu wasn't much help when you were getting shot at by someone you couldn't even see.

He raised the rifle to his shoulder and veered the barrel over the distant sand. The white emptiness of the dunes was unbroken. He spun round at the sound of approaching horses. Galloping straight for them, horses splashing through the sand, was a pack of twelve Mexicans.

'Can you use a gun?' Sloane asked.

'Sure,' said Billy.

'Here . . .' Sloane drew his Colt Dragoon and pressed the butt into the Chinaman's free hand.

One of the Mexicans was big and broad under a sombrero wide as a wagon wheel. He made a nice fat target. Sloane took aim.

'*Hola, Amigos!*' the lead rider called out, rearing his horse. He threw up one arm in a friendly gesture. 'Do not shoot – we are your friends!'

The rest of the riders reined in behind their leader. So far none of them had drawn their pistols. Sloane lowered the rifle but kept it pointed, finger tight on trigger. He swerved the barrel briefly in the direction of Joe's body.

'This a taste of your friendship?' he called.

The leader of the Mexicans danced closer on a frisky blood-bay pony. His affable grin was in contrast to the unsmiling faces of his men behind him.

'We were out chasing stray horses, señores, when we heard the sound of a gun . . . Your friend – he is hurt bad, señor?'

'He's dead,' said Sloane.

'I am sorry to hear that, señor. That is a big pity . . .'

The Mexican swung round and shouted an order to his men in rapid Spanish. Eight men detached themselves from the group of horsemen and rode off in the direction from which the gunshot had come. They were led by the big man in the wide sombrero. The Mexican on the bay wheeled back to face Sloane and Billy.

'It is sure to have been the men of El Muerte,' he said, 'or perhaps that *negrito loco* that hunts the heads of men . . .'

Sloane lowered his stare to Joe's body, the first chance he'd had to take a long close look. Joe's head was smashed open like a broken egg.

'It wasn't the bone-devil,' said Sloane. 'He wouldn't have thrown away two dollars and fifty cents that easy.'

The leader of the Mexicans reined in beside the two Americans. 'Permit me – I am Manuel Aguilar. And you must be that gringo I have heard so much about. The one who made angels of Pancho Gonzalez and his cousins.'

Aguilar bared his teeth in a grin that proclaimed his admiration. His was an arrogantly handsome face, lighter in shade than most Mexicans for he was a *paisano*, with hardly any Indian blood in his veins. He wore neatly-trimmed moustachios curling down around easy-smiling, sensuous lips. His dark, laughing eyes and assured manner suggested a shrewd intelligence.

'If you say so,' said Sloane.

Aguilar laughed. 'You are modest, señor. That is good in a man.' Aguilar's eyes switched to Billy. 'And this is your *compadre* – a great fighter also . . . señores, I know it would make my *patron* very much happy if you would accompany me to his *hacienda*.'

'That's fine,' said Sloane. 'But we're not looking for your *patron* – we're looking for El Muerte.'

'I know that, señores. Who has not heard of the gringos who look for El Muerte? It is about this very matter that my *patron* wishes to speak with you . . .'

'Who is this *patron* of your's?'

Aguilar beamed broadly. 'A very important man around here, señor. Perhaps you have heard of him – Don Luis Fernando de Silviera y Castilia!'

Billy Wang looked quickly over at Sloane. But Sloane's face betrayed no surprise at the name.

'If he's that important, I guess we'll just have to go and see what he wants,' he said dryly.

As he spoke, the men Aguilar had sent after Joe's killer returned in a boil of dust.

'What news, Toro?' Aguilar demanded of the big man in the sombrero. 'Did you find the one that did this thing?' He motioned with his head towards Joe's body.

'We saw a man riding away,' said Toro, his voice coarse and harsh. 'We chased him but the sonovabitch was too far ahead and lost us.'

Toro had a massive brigandish face, swarthy as an Indian's. From beneath his jutting nose, fierce black moustachios dangled down to his chin.

'Where was he heading, this one you could not catch?'

'Towards the camp of El Muerte,' the big man answered.

Aguilar nodded thoughtfully, his suspicions confirmed. 'As I thought,' he said. 'El Muerte again. Always El Muerte!'

Sloane had joined Billy beside Joe's body. He looked down at the dead Irishman, his face becoming hard as gunmetal. All his life Joe had been robbed of the things he'd wanted and now he'd been robbed of the chance to die like a man. He'd wanted to make a final stand, to go out with a last grand, defiant gesture. Instead, he'd been slapped down by a bushwhacker's bullet – fired by a man whose face he'd never seen. One more good reason to catch up with El Muerte.

Sloane knelt beside the body and emptied Joe's pockets. He found some dollar bills, a few letters from a girl, yellowed with age, and a fistful of cigars.

'No sense in wasting good cigars,' he said and transferred the stogies to his own pocket.

He gave Joe's rifle to Billy. He already had something in his rifle-case – though it wasn't a rifle.

They buried Joe where he'd fallen. There was no marker to put over the grave like he'd wanted so they just laid his hat on top and weighed it down with a rock. Sloane told himself that some day he'd return and mark the spot with something more permanent. But he knew he never would.

The *hacienda* of Don Luis Fernando de Silviera y Castilia was an oasis of fertility. Date palms swayed and figs grew plump and ripe. Trees were bright with every kind of fruit. Cattle grazed on pasture so green it hurt eyes grown used to the colourless glare of the desert lands. At the heart of this lush empire was the residence of Don Luis – an imposing two-storey block of stucco-covered adobe with a gallery running all the way round it. Adjoining the main building was a second smaller adobe dwelling. In addition there were several wooden outbuildings where the *vaqueros* and other ranch-hands lived.

On a strip of bare ground running between the *casa* and an exotically flowered garden, a dark cannon crouched like a massively alert iron watch-dog warning off intruders from its master's home. The cannon appeared clean, well-oiled and ready for use. A pyramid of sleek black cannon-balls was stacked handily alongside the gaping sentinel.

'That's quite a pea-shooter Don Luis' got himself,' Sloane

observed as they rode towards the *hacienda* in the red glow of the setting sun. 'Does it work?'

'Of course, señor Sloane,' Aguilar confirmed. 'Is this not Mexico? In the Republic, guns are silent only when they are being reloaded.'

Aguilar had sent a rider ahead to alert Don Luis of their arrival. The grandee was waiting for them.

Everything about Don Luis from the silver hair brushed back from the high brow of his sensitive face to the exquisite cut and gold facings of his black velvet suit reflected the nobility of his birth. He could trace his descent from a long line of Spanish aristocrats that stretched unbroken to the *Conquistadores* and beyond – and he delighted in doing so at length for the benefit of those he considered worthy enough to share this privileged knowledge. He was not a large man but there was pride enough in his upright manner and in the sharp angles of his hawkish face to make do for the largest of men. He stepped forward to meet the white man and the yellow man when they dismounted.

'Welcome, señor Sloane – and you too, señor Wang. I am honoured that you have consented to visit my home.'

As he spoke, Don Luis' eyes roamed over the ragged, trail-dusted and otherwise filthy appearance of his guests. The keen dark eyes in his patrician face betrayed something other than honour. Don Luis dismissed Aguilar and his men and led Sloane and Billy inside into a white hallway lined with portraits of long-dead men all wearing the same expression of challenging hautiness as Don Luis himself.

'I wish to speak with you on a matter of great importance,' he told Sloane. 'But I see you have had a long and no doubt tiring journey. We dine in one hour. In the meantime, hot baths and a change of clothes will be made available if you wish . . . *Manolo!*'

As he shouted the name, Don Luis clapped his hands sharply together, once. Within seconds, a dark-faced servant in a white jacket was hurrying towards them, trying hard to give the impression that he wasn't running.

'Manolo, show these gentlemen to their rooms and see to their requirements.'

'Yes, señor,' said Manolo, dipping his head.

Manolo led the way up a flight of stairs. Sloane and Billy followed.

'I look forward to the pleasure of your company at dinner,' said Don Luis graciously, his eyes following them up the stairs.

Sloane wondered what in Hell could be so important to a man like Don Luis that he had to grit his teeth and be nice to a pair of dusty saddle-tramps. He thought about that as he lay soaking the dirt from his bones in a hot steaming tub. Later, when he'd towelled himself dry, he found that Manolo had left a set of clean clothes on the bed and whisked his own stained garments into a cupboard where they could offend no one but the moths. The clothes were a good fit. Sloane watched his reflection grinning at him from the wardrobe mirror as he stood before it in the ruffled silk shirt and suit of ruby velvet. He grinned back.

Soon after, Manolo appeared and respectfully announced that dinner was served. Sloane met Billy as he emerged from his room. They smiled at the sight of each others' spanking clean duds.

Don Luis was waiting for them in the dining room along with Aguilar. Aguilar had also traded his riding clothes for a clean shirt and suit and he cut as fine a figure as his master. If the sight of the two Americans dressed up like gentlemen amused them, they managed to restrict their amusement to a gleam in the eye.

There was another person in the room – a young attractive girl of about nineteen. Her face, framed by a black lace *rebozo*, had the shyness and delicate beauty of a madonna. She wore a high-collared dress that didn't quite succeed in disguising the ripening charms it contained. The girl looked at the two strangers with demure fascination.

'My daughter Rosalia,' Done Luis informed them in a voice brimming with paternal affection. 'My dear – señor Sloane and señor Wang...'

She curtsied and held out her hand for them to kiss. Don Luis watched concernedly to see if the heathen Chinaman would brush his lips against her fingers as was politely expected of a gentleman – or whether he would sink his teeth ravenously into her pale wrist. Billy disappointed him.

They sat round an ornately-laid candlelit table and ate rich spicy food served on silver platters. There was steak, turkey and salads and *enchiladas* and many things to which Sloane couldn't put a name.

As they ate, Don Luis made polite conversation. He spoke spiritedly of the victories over the French and their mercenary army and of his own part in the struggle. His own efforts had not been satisfactorily recognised he told them. He had expected a part in the government at least. If that tyrant Juarez had not jumped in and forced himself on the people as President – *Quién sabe*?

Sloane paid little attention to the nobleman's talk. He'd come to hear about one thing only – El Muerte. Several times during the meal he caught Rosalia throwing discreet searching glances in his direction. Each time he found her out, she chastely downcast her eyes, veiling them beneath long silky lashes.

After they had eaten, coffee and brandy were served. His thin, uncalloused hands curled round the bowl of his glass, Don Luis settled back in his chair and fixed his imperious gaze on Sloane.

'We have heard with much amazement the story of your fight with the bandit Pancho Gonzalez and his cousins,' he confided. 'It is hard to believe this story. Aguilar has suggested that there were not twenty bandits as the story tells but perhaps only one or two bandits . . .'

'Don't matter none to Pancho Gonzalez what Mister Aguilar thinks,' said Sloane coldly and drained his glass.

'That is true,' Don Luis smiled, 'and since he cannot tell us himself what happened we must find some other way of establishing the truth.' He clapped his hands and rapped out an order that sent Manolo scurrying from the room. Then he proceeded to study his glass in silence.

A few moments later Manolo returned with the big moustachioed *mestizo* known as Toro. Toro had obviously been hanging around outside awaiting his master's summons. His massive body was bared to the waist revealing solid ridges of muscle. Without his great sombrero, his matted hair hung lankly to his shoulders. Toro bowed his head briefly to Don Luis then stood his ground a short way from the table, arms folded, legs apart. He glared at Sloane. Sloane and the Chinaman looked to Don Luis for an explanation.

'Toro is the best fighter on the *hacienda*,' the aristocrat told them. 'He has broken the backs of so many men that no one will fight with him any more. This makes Toro unhappy because he loves to fight – and it makes us unhappy because it gives us pleasure to watch him enjoying himself . . .'

Aguilar leaned over to Sloane and whispered to him in a leering voice, low so that Rosalia could not hear: 'He is called Toro because for strength he eats the *cojones* of the bull – the testicles!'

'Señor Sloane,' began Don Luis in an eager cajoling voice, 'I would consider it an honour if you would demonstrate to us your great skill by fighting with Toro.'

Sloane stared evenly at Don Luis, his face a mask. 'I'm no prize-fighter,' he said finally. 'I don't fight a man unless I got a good reason.'

'That Don Luis asks you this thing – is that not a good enough reason?' Aguilar asked soothingly.

'No,' said Sloane.

Aguilar lost his brilliant smile. 'Perhaps he was a sick man, this Pancho Gonzalez,' he said insinuatingly. 'Perhaps he was a cripple!'

Sloane impaled the Mexican on the end of his steely gaze.

'Please, Señor Sloane . . .' Rosalia appealed, her eyes wide and pleading, 'I would like to see you fight. Will you not do this thing for me?'

'There you are, Señor Sloane,' said Don Luis lightly. 'You cannot refuse the request of a young lady . . .'

Sloane could. He looked up at Toro's swarthy face. 'I'd like to hear what the man I'm s'posed to fight has to say about it.'

Toro bared his teeth in a snarling grimace. 'Pancho Gonzalez has many cousins,' he growled, 'I am one of them.' He spread his huge hands before him for them all to see. 'With these hands I will tear you to pieces, gringo . . . One piece for each of my cousins you have dishonoured!'

A tired smile tugged at the edges of Sloane's mouth. 'Now that's what I call a good reason,' he said.

The two men squared off in front of the *casa*, under the one-eyed gaze of the cannon. Don Luis stood watching them, one hand resting on Rosalia's shoulder. She had put on a shawl which she pulled close around her for the warmth of the evening had given way to the crisp chill of night. Close by stood Billy and Aguilar. Manolo and several *vaqueros* held flaming torches which threw an unsteady light on the two men who were going to fight each other.

Sloane had stripped off his shirt and jacket. In the dancing glare of the torches, his sinewy body was bronze. He faced the big dark-faced Mexican and waited for him to make his move. Toro watched Sloane with the same pleasure as a hungry thief eyeing an unguarded chicken. This was going to be easy, he thought. Enjoyably easy. He was so obviously superior to the gringo in both weight and strength.

With a bestial growl, Toro launched himself at Sloane, the fingers of his big hands stretching for Sloane's throat. Sloane watched his approach with bored disdain as if it was the least interesting thing in the whole world. Then, when the big man reached him, he side-stepped – neat as a toreador escaping the horns of a bull. One foot lashed out and swept Toro's feet from under him. The hulking Mexican toppled and tasted dirt. He didn't like the taste. He spat grit from his mouth and clambered to his feet, glowering furiously at Sloane. His heaving anger flared his nostrils. It made him look like the animal whose name he shared. Watching him, Sloane half-expected the Mexican to paw the ground with a hoof, lower his head and charge. He didn't paw the ground but he lowered his head and he charged, aiming to butt Sloane off his feet. He got as far as Sloane's rising boot. The spinning crescent kick tossed him back to the ground.

Toro's next attack was more cautious. Big hands defensively raised, he closed on Sloane with the slow wariness of a man trying to ease past a frothing-mad dog. But when Sloane's foot rose to meet him, he moved with the speed of a striking snake. He seized the booted foot two-handed and used it as a lever to slam Sloane against the ground. Then he threw himself on top of the American, covering him with his crushing weight. The heel of one hand pressed against Sloane's chin, fingers hooking for his eyes. He laughed as he forced Sloane's head back at a neck-breaking angle. Sloane's knee hammered his groin. The big Mex roared. The sickening pain flashed through his body, forcing him to relax his hold for a brief instant. Just long enough for Sloane to snap straight his leg and send Toro hurtling from him.

When the Mexican staggered upright, Sloane was waiting for him. Toro reeled under the pulverising impact of a flurry of hammer-fisted blows. His own return punches were swiftly blocked and slammed aside. But Toro wasn't through yet. As a dragon's-head fist streaked at his face, he grabbed hold of Sloane's wrist and hauled him forward onto the receiving end of a fierce elbow slam. Before Sloane could recover, Toro wrapped both beefy arms round Sloane's neck in a deadly embrace. He held on tight, dragging Sloane back and forth in his choking grip.

Two rigid knife-hand strikes gouged deeply into the soft flesh beneath Toro's ribs. Toro gasped, suddenly breathless with pain. Sloane slipped out from under the slackened grip, wailing a loud inhuman *Ki-Ai* yell as he swung round and sent a roundhouse kick smashing against Toro's head. He pressed his advantage, advancing relentlessly on the dazed retreating Mexican. Punches pounded against Toro fast as rain. Fists hailed against his face, kicks thundered into his body.

Toro swayed groggily, struggling to keep on his feet. Sloane leapt up and delivered a straight-arrow flying-kick that sent Toro sprawling backwards. The big man barrelled into two torch-holding *vaqueros*, carrying them with him to the ground. The torches flew spinning through the air and flickered out. None of the three men in the tangled heap moved. Sloane sucked blood from his grazed knuckles.

Don Luis strode up, his face full of enthusiastic approval.

'Excellent, Señor Sloane,' he said. 'You have proved to us that all we have heard is true. If I had not seen these things with my own eyes, I would not have believed them.'

Sloane inclined his head modestly. Behind Don Luis he could see Rosalia watching him. Her coy eyes were bright with admiration. From beside her, Aguilar stepped forward. He handed Sloane his shirt and jacket and added his own enthusiastic congratulations, grinning so much Sloane could see the teeth in the back of his head. *Vaqueros* were gathered round Toro like bees round a honey pot. Billy Wang strolled over from the direction of the activity.

'All three out cold! Not bad, Sloane,' he reluctantly admitted. 'Not bad at all.'

Billy turned to Don Luis and Aguilar. 'Of course, if you want to see some real good Chinese boxing,' he told them, 'you have to come to a real Chinaman.'

'I look forward to that future pleasure,' said Don Luis with a slight bow of the head. 'But now my daughter and I must go to the chapel and give thanks to God for sending to us a man such as Señor Sloane . . .'

'Don't thank God – thank El Muerte,' said Sloane.

'Then for once good has come of evil,' said the hawk-faced aristocrat. 'Thank you, Señor Sloane, for permitting us to see your skill as a fighter. Tomorrow we will talk further of El Muerte.'

Don Luis bowed crisply then turned and joined Rosalia. He escorted her back towards the *casa*. Sloane watched them. As they made their way towards the house it seemed to him that Don Luis' hand slipped momentarily from Rosalia's waist to caress the firm curves that lay beneath. Aguilar followed his gaze to see what held Sloane's interest.

'There's nothing like a father's love for his daughter,' said Sloane thoughtfully.

Aguilar looked uncomfortable. He had to put a lot of effort into his smile. 'They are a close family, señor,' he said. 'Come, I will show you to your room.'

After he'd cleaned up his cuts and bruises, Sloane lay on the soft bed they'd given him with his hands behind his head and thought about a few things. Like why Don Luis had been so all-fired anxious to see him fight. And what the link was between the aristocrat and El Muerte. He was still lying there thinking when there was a knock on his door. A low secretive knock.

It was Rosalia. But not the demure madonna-like Rosalia he'd seen earlier. It wasn't coyness Sloane saw in her brown eyes now that she stood before him in something silky and lacy that revealed more than it hid. Without a *rebozo* her long night-black hair flowed freely down over bare shoulders. She looked up at him and smiled, the provoking smile of a woman who knows exactly what she has to offer a man.

She had a lot of nerve, Sloane thought, and nerve wasn't all she had a lot of. She was nervously playing with the chain of a silver crucifix dangling from her neck. The crucifix stroked the deep cleft of her breasts forcing Sloane to take notice of them – not that he needed encouragement.

'Isn't it kinda late for little girls to be out of bed?' Sloane asked her.

Rosalia lowered her eyes. She watched the crucifix bobbing between her dark breasts. 'But I'm a big girl, Señor Sloane,' she said. Sloane was looking the same place she was. 'I can see that,' he said. 'Any special reason for this visit or is it all part of the room service?'

She raised her eyes to his. They were dark and bright as polished oak. 'I wanted to tell you that I am glad you're here, Señor Sloane . . . It can be very lonely out here.' Her voice was hushed and girlish. 'Perhaps you feel that way too. I cannot sleep and I lie awake . . . My room – it is opposite your's – down the passage-way a little . . .'

Her smile said *drop by any time*. Sloane looked down at her young inviting face without emotion. As he looked, he listened. He heard – the shivering whisper of spurs – the sudden exhalation of breath of someone who was doing a bad job of giving up breathing.

He said: 'Thanks for telling me where your room is, señorita. I'll be real careful not to go into it by mistake.'

Her red lips fell open. Her angry eyes snapped at him like castanets. 'You do not find me desirable?'

Sloane roved his gaze over her body. It was a good place for sight-seeing. Sure, he found her desirable. But not as desirable as staying alive. He reached out and touched her bare arm. Her skin felt soft and warm beneath his hand. He slid his hand up her arm to her shoulder. She trembled slightly and her breath grew thick. She closed her eyes and tilted her head towards his, her lips waiting.

'Taking another man's stray is the same as rustling,' he told her. 'You can get hung for both.' Then he pushed her out of the room and closed the door.

She stood there for a time in front of the closed door, eyes blazing and lips quivering. Then she tossed back her hair and flounced down the corridor towards her room. An arm blocked her path.

The arm belonged to Aguilar. He grinned toothily at her. 'That gringo is a smart man,' he said. 'Very smart. But you – you are not smart and soon I will be dancing on your belly. . .'

He dipped his head to find her lips. He found instead the stinging palm of her hand across his cheek. Pressing a hand to the burning pain he grinned as she retreated angrily to her room. The memory of the pain would sweeten his pleasure when she was his to do with as he wanted.

Don Luis sent for Sloane in the morning. Manolo ushered him into the aristocrat's study, a spacious sun-filled room smelling of wood and leather. Don Luis rose from behind a wide desk and greeted him. He gestured for Sloane to take a seat.

'Cigar?' Don Luis offered, pushing a box across the desk.

'I got my own,' said Sloane, drawing one of Joe's stogies from his breast pocket. He put it to his lips and leaned forward to accept a light from Don Luis. Puffing, he settled back in the chair and waited for the proud-faced Spaniard to do some explaining. He had a lot of it to do.

Don Luis paced the room, his lips pursed, his hands clasped regally behind his back. Whatever he had to say, he wasn't finding it easy, Sloane observed.

'There is much I must tell you, Señor Sloane,' the aristocrat began, his voice earnest, 'and I must ask that you be patient with me for my story begins many years ago – almost thirty years now – yet I remember the events of those days as if they happened only last week. You are still young, Señor Sloane, but I can see you are a man of experience, a man who has seen and felt much. I do not have to tell you how a man may change many times in his life.'

As he spoke, Don Luis walked over to one of the windows in the room. 'We are as clay in the hands of God, Señor. The woman we love today – we may hate tomorrow. So it is with much else in life I have found. We change from year to year. The idealism of our youth dies many deaths.' Don Luis swung away from the window and turned his gaze on Sloane. 'When I was young, Señor Sloane, I believed in the Revolution. Not the revolution of a bandit like Juarez but a revolution that would make Mexico strong again and all her people happy. Liberty for all! That was my promise. How I believed in that word *libertad!* I was prepared to kill for it – and I did many times. Too many times . . .'

Don Luis shook his head, his face bitter with regret. 'But there is only one such time about which I must tell you. With my *vaqueros* I was hunting for some men I believed to be my enemies – *guerrilleros* who were fighting against us. We followed them to the mission at Lascara. In those days I hated the Church as men hate a tyrant. We attacked the mission. We killed everyone there that we found. It did not matter if they were priests or women or children – they had to die for the Revolution!'

Don Luis sighed wearily, a sound of disgust. He stared once more out of the window. Something he saw seemed to hold his attention. The silence lengthened.

'Go on,' said Sloane.

Don Luis turned to face him. 'You cannot imagine with what shame I tell you of these horrors,' he said. 'I would give anything that they had not happened. But what is done is done. The past cannot be changed as easily as what a man believes . . . I can still remember the screams of the children, the wails of the women as my men fell upon them. These things I will always remember.'

Don Luis walked across the room and sank into the chair behind his desk. He looked across the desk at Sloane with tired eyes. 'You have heard of the crystal skull of Lascara?' he asked.

'I've heard,' said Sloane.

'The priests say it is a holy relic but I saw only its beauty not its holiness – beauty that seemed more of the Devil than of God. When I saw it I felt as a boy who desires his first woman. I wanted it – and so I took it. Señor Sloane, I am no longer the same man as him who killed those people so that they could be liberated. I am not that same man who took the skull from the altar in the mission. I no longer believe in the Revolution. Why fight to give votes to peasants if all they can do with their votes is elect some cut-throat like Juarez? No, Señor Sloane, to be strong Mexico needs strong men with strong ideas. And strong men need a strong God . . .'

There was a portrait of the Madonna and her child hanging from the wall of Don Luis' study. The aristocrat looked up at the portrait. He seemed to draw strength from it. 'Once I hated the Church and its priests. Now I love the Church as I love my own mother.'

His gaze shifted to Sloane. 'When I returned to the bosom of the Church my soul was stained with sin as my hands were stained with the blood of innocents. I have made payment for those sins, Señor Sloane. I have paid many times over. I have paid with gold so that masses are said every day for the souls of those killed by my men. I have paid for candles to be lit in their honour – hundreds of candles, thousands! And after all I have done, all I have paid, do you think those priests at the mission can find it in their compassionate hearts to forgive a sinner?'

Don Luis shook his head, his shoulders shaking with suppressed anger. 'No, Señor Sloane, they cannot! They refuse to forgive me. Me, who has given them so much . . . They withold from me the forgiveness they would give to a common *bandido*!'

He leaned urgently across the desk towards Sloane, close enough so Sloane could see the fear in Don Luis' eyes. It wasn't fear of men or even of death – but of what came after death.

'Señor Sloane, I am a believer. I believe in Hell and its torments, I believe in its everlasting fires which roast the souls of sinners . . . I do not want to go to Hell – and those pigs of priests refuse to forgive my sins, refuse to give me Absolution unless . . .' The words trailed off in his throat. Don Luis' face was full of despair at the thought of Hell. He swallowed heavily.

'Unless?'

'Unless I return the holy skull to the mission!'

Sloane shrugged. 'So give it back to 'em,' he said.

'Two years ago,' Don Luis told him slowly, dejectedly, 'the skull was stolen from me – by El Muerte!'

Sloane nodded, a faint smile on his lips. The pieces were all fitting together. He understood. 'And you want me to go after him and bring the skull back for you so's you can go to heaven?'

The aristocrat made a despairing gesture with his hands. 'Who else can I turn to?' He rose from behind his desk and strolled over to the window before speaking again.

'My men are too afraid of El Muerte's reputation to go after him. Some of them actually believe that he is a dead man who has returned to life. The government troops leave him alone because he is a hero to the people . . .'

He turned back to Sloane, an appeal in his eyes. 'But you . . . You are not afraid of him. You wish to kill him – and the way you fight I believe you have a chance. I ask of you that at the same time you return to me the crystal skull.'

Sloane leaned over and crushed to death the butt of his cigar on the smooth polished surface of Don Luis' desk. He rose to leave.

'Thanks for askin', Don Luis, but I'm not lookin' for any jobs right now . . .'

'I'm sorry to hear you say that, Señor Sloane,' said the Spaniard.

'Life's full of little disappointments,' said Sloane making for the door.

When he next spoke Don Luis' voice was harsher, the words coming fast and confident. 'I am sorry because now I shall have to ask you to look out of this window and see what will happen if you do not do as I wish!'

Sloane stopped in his tracks. He slowly turned to face the aristocrat. The way Don Luis had spoken he expected him to have a gun in his hand. He didn't. His smug expression suggested he had something better than a gun up his sleeve. Sloane crossed the room and joined Don Luis at the window. He looked out.

The window gave a good view of the smaller adobe building next to the *casa*. He noticed for the first time that the windows of the building were barred like a jail. On the balcony of the building, between two grim guards aiming rifles stood the dainty figure of a Chinese girl, her pretty face filled with fear.

It was Su Fan.

CHAPTER NINE

'*You bastard!*'

Sloane spun towards Don Luis, his face ablaze with anger. The Spaniard raised his hand meaningfully. Sloane looked into the prim black mouth of a Deringer ·42. The sight of the small elegant gold-handled pistol brought an ugly smile to his lips. He judged the distance for a kick.

'Please, Señor Sloane,' the Spaniard warned him impatiently. 'I have no doubt you can take this gun from me with one of your tricks. But think first of the girl – my men have orders to kill her the moment you offer me violence.'

Sloane's hands were fists primed to explode into punches. But the thought of danger to Su Fan made him hold his attack. He swung away from the dapper aristocrat, back towards the window. The two *vaqueros* on the opposite balcony were holding their rifles to Su Fan's head and their expressions meant business. Su Fan saw Sloane. She called out to him, her voice high and strained.

Sloane turned quickly back to Don Luis. 'What's your price?' he snarled.

'Only what I have told you, señor. Return the skull to me and the girl goes free.'

'And if I don't get it back?'

The Spaniard shrugged regretfully. 'Then she dies.'

The look in Don Luis' face was coldly fanatical. Sloane had no doubt he meant what he said. He pushed back the surge of impotent fury that heaved his chest. He felt like smashing his fist into the wall. Or Don Luis' face.

'I thought El Muerte had her,' he said. 'What's she doin' here?'

'My men came across some of El Muerte's *bandidos* . . .

There was a fight. The bandits escaped but they left something behind – her!'

'Careless of 'em,' said Sloane.

'But very convenient for me. And now I suggest you go, Señor Sloane. It is a long ride to Lascara. There is a report from one of my men that he was in the village last night. He may still be there. And wherever he goes, he takes the skull with him.'

Sloane looked back at the balcony. It was empty. 'How 'bout the Chinaman?' he asked.

'He may go with you or stay as you wish. But warn him not to attempt anything foolish. There will be two of my men with her at all times. She will be the first one to die if anyone tries to rescue her.'

'How do I know you won't kill her anyway?' Sloane asked. 'Even if I get the skull?'

Don Luis looked seriously pained.

'I am a man of honour, señor. You have my word as a Spaniard, as a gentleman.'

'Sure,' said Sloane, turning to leave, heading for the door. 'I was forgettin' you were a man of honour.'

'Don't disappoint me, Señor Sloane,' Don Luis cautioned, raising his voice. 'I very much want to go to Heaven.'

Sloane paused in the doorway, contempt in his face. 'Somethin' tells me you won't find many friends up there,' he said then slammed out of the room.

He passed Rosalia on the stairs. When she saw the look in his face, she drew back. Fast. Sloane made straight for Billy Wang's room. The young Chinaman was gouging the air with fingers hooked into claws – practising his tiger stance. Sloane told him what had happened.

'Su Fan here?' said Billy incredulously. His surprise quickly became joy. 'Let's go get her!'

'They'll kill her,' said Sloane. It was a statement of fact. 'You got a choice – you come with me or you stay.'

Billy pressed a fist against his palm, his face tight with concentration.

'How're we gonna get the skull off El Muerte?'

'I was figurin' on askin' him for it,' said Sloane wryly.

The Chinaman looked at him like he'd gone screaming crazy.

'You got any better ideas?' Sloane asked him.

'I'm staying,' Billy decided.

'Good,' said Sloane. 'You'd only get in my way.'

Billy glared at him.

'She'll need someone to get her out of here – I don't think you'll be comin' back alive.'

'You're real encouraging,' said Sloane, turning to leave.

'She's my woman, Sloane,' Billy called after him. 'Don't you forget it!'

Sloane looked back at him, his face a mask. He said, 'Right now she ain't nobody's woman but Don Luis'.'

Back in his room Sloane ripped off the velvet jacket and ruffled shirt. He put on his own sweat-stained shirt and the filthy blood-splashed suit that had once been white. He felt cleaner wearing them than the fancy new clothes Don Luis had given him.

He saddled his horse and rode out.

Leaning over a corral fence, Toro and Aguilar watched him. Toro only half-watched him because one of his eyes was swollen closed in a purple bruised face.

'Bring back two heads, señor,' Aguilar called out, 'the death's head and the head of El Muerte!'

Aguilar laughed but Toro did not. He would have liked to but his face hurt too much. Both men knew the gringo would never come back. Either he would run and hide like any sensible man. Or he would die.

If Sloane heard Aguilar's laughter, his face did not show it. He laid heels to the Morgan, heading for Lascara. In the distance, he saw a pack of *vaqueros* exercising the *remuda*.

It could be the glare of the sun playing tricks with his eyes he thought – but it seemed to him that the herd of horses was chasing after a bright golden streak of sunshine.

Through the barred windows of her prison, Su Fan watched Sloane ride out. She watched until he merged with the horizon, until she could no longer see him. Her jade eyes misted with tears. Earlier, when she'd seen Sloane at the window, she'd almost wept with joy. She thought he'd come to pay a ransom or make some other kind of deal that would get her released. She'd waited and waited for him to come and take her away. But he hadn't shown. And now he was riding out. Without her.

She couldn't understand it. She'd tried asking the guards but they'd just laughed at her, undressing her with their eyes as usual. Chiquita, the girl who brought her meals had told her there was another stranger in the *hacienda*. A yellow man, she'd said. A Chinaman. Chiquita had said he was young and not bad looking for a man who was the colour of a piece of cheese. It sounded like Billy Wang. Su Fan's heart hammered when she thought of that name. She feared and hated him – hated him almost as much as the killers who'd butchered her parents before her eyes.

He'd seemed pleasant enough when he first started working for Chang Fung. Eager to please he'd worked hard and always with a smile on his face. Then he began to get interested in her. Too interested. She'd told him that there was someone else, someone she was waiting for. She'd told him about Sloane. He'd called her names because she loved someone not of her own people. Then, one night when she'd gone to the well to fetch water, he'd attacked her, tried to force himself on her. Chang Fung had heard her screams. He'd come running, waving his sword, and chased Billy away. Before he left Billy had threatened them with the power of the Tongs, the secret societies that ruled the Chinese community in San Francisco with an iron fist of terror. He'd promised that his uncle's Tong would send assassins to kill Chang Fung. Her father had laughed and swiped at him with the flat edge of his sword. Billy ran off. She'd seen him a few times after that, lurking around the house, waiting for a chance to get at her. And now it looked like he'd followed her all the way to Mexico for his revenge.

Su Fan moved from the window, hiding her tears from the guards behind a mask of anger. The fat guard called Carlos scrambled back from the sudden movement. He knew what had happened to Alfonso when he'd come too close to the yellow she-devil. She'd kicked him hard in the parts that made him a man. It would be weeks before he could even look at a pretty woman again without pain. Carlos retreated until he felt the wall at his back. Beside him stood Pedro, tall and silent. Together the two guards watched the despair of the fragile-faced Chinese girl, their eyes and their rifle-barrels following her as she paced helplessly inside the small locked room.

Father Josef reined in, bringing the buckboard to a groaning halt outside the mission. Almost immediately the buckboard was surrounded by squealing children admiring the coffin that the priest had brought back from the next village. It was a good coffin. Pascual the coffin-maker would go to his final rest in a better coffin than he had ever made in his whole life.

Father Josef sprang down from the wagon. He shook the dust from his cassock as a woman shakes crumbs from her skirt. When he looked up Father Francesco had emerged from the mission, drawn outside by the cries of the children. The older priest looked joylessly at the coffin in the back of the wagon.

'A fine coffin,' he said without enthusiasm. 'A pity you brought only one.'

107

Father Josef looked sharply at his fellow priest, a question in his eyes.

'It would have saved you a journey if you had brought back more,' Father Francesco told him.

'How many more?'

'Three,' replied the older priest. 'José the *pulque*-vendor, his daughter Consuela and the old *vaquero*, Horacio.'

Father Josef clutched at the buckboard for support. 'El Muerte?' he asked in a tired voice.

Father Francesco nodded. 'They came last night. He has ordered that the village honours him with a feast on the Day of the Dead.'

'Is there no news of the Americanos?' Father Josef asked with a faint hope.

'One is dead. Perhaps all three.'

The young priest lowered his head. He stood in that position for a long silent moment, his face working as he listened to the words of his heart.

'We can only pray that God sends us help,' said Father Francesco bleakly.

Father Josef raised his eyes to the older man. They were fired by a new fierce determination.

'God helps those who help themselves,' he said firmly, resolutely.

His face set with purpose he moved past Father Francesco and entered the mission. When he came out again there was a bandolier of bullets slung over his shoulder, and in his hand he carried an ancient rifle. Father Francesco watched him, speechless.

The younger priest approached the buckboard. He laid a hand on the coffin. 'We will need four more coffins,' he said. 'This one is for El Muerte.'

Hours later, Father Francesco was still praying for the soul of the misguided priest when a panting boy tugged urgently at his cassock and told him there was a stranger, near the mission, a tall gringo. The priest ran towards the man on the horse, calling out for him to wait. Sloane waited.

'A terrible thing, Señor Sloane,' said Father Francesco breathlessly when he'd caught up.

'Father Josef has gone to kill El Muerte . . . a priest and he goes to break the Lord's Commandments!'

'Guess he found he was more of a man than a priest,' said Sloane. He'd liked the eager little priest with the bright eyes.

'Please, señor, bring him back! Do not let him die with sinful thoughts.'

Sloane looked down into the imploring face of Father Francesco. 'I'll bring him back,' he said. 'If there's anythin' left to bring back.'

He put heels to his horse and followed the deep-grooved trail of the buckboard into the land of death.

Billy Wang sprang from his chair, snapping instantly into a defensive position when someone suddenly entered his room. It was Rosalia.

Billy relaxed, grinning. 'Guess I'm jumpy tonight,' he apologised.

Rosalia put a finger to her lips, cautioning him to silence. She stood stock-still by the open door, listening. Then, satisfied she had not been followed, she closed the door.

Frowning, Billy watched the girl cross the room and sit down on his bed. Her face was unsmiling, purposeful. He saw a strength in her he had not noticed before.

'The Chinese girl Don Fernando is holding hostage – do you want to help her escape?' she asked. She spoke urgently, her voice hushed as if afraid of being overheard.

Billy hesitated to answer.

'You can trust me,' Rosalia assured him.

'Sure I want to help her escape,' said Billy. 'I want to get her as far away from here as I can.'

109

Rosalia nodded. 'Good. I will help you – if you help me escape from here also.'

Bewilderment showed in Billy's face. 'But you're Don Luis' daughter . . .'

Rosalia laughed, a hard scornful laugh. 'Don Luis has no real daughters,' she told him, 'but there are many girls he calls his daughters. When he tires of them he gives them to his men to play with. I have been his daughter for five months now. A woman knows when a man begins to lose interest in her. Soon he will be looking for a new girl to be his daughter. Then he will give me to Aguilar. And when Aguilar has finished with me he will give me to that brute Toro.'

She shuddered. 'I would rather die.'

Billy looked at her thoughtfully. 'How about the guards? They've got orders to kill her if there's any trouble.'

'I know how to take care of the guards,' said Rosalia. 'But we must act soon. Tomorrow!'

'What's the hurry?'

'Once a month an Americano called Sullivan comes with a wagonload of guns and ammunition for Don Luis. The guns are for the army he hopes to raise to fight against the Juaristas. In exchange Don Luis gives to Sullivan young girls who are sold to rich men across the border.'

'Guns for girls . . . not a bad trade,' Billy admitted.

'I have heard Don Luis say he will give the Chinese girl to Sullivan. The day after tomorrow it is the Day of the Dead in Mexico. Sullivan is due here by then.'

'So it has to be tomorrow . . .'

'Yes. Don Luis will not let you live after the Day of the Dead.'

'He sure is a hospitable man,' said Billy easily. 'What's your plan?'

Rosalia told him. Afterwards, she left the room taking care not to be seen. Don Luis was waiting for her in bed, naked beneath the crisp sheets.

'Where have you been?' he asked in a voice taut with displeasure.

'I went to the chapel – to pray that Sloane will return safely with the skull.'

As she spoke, Rosalia hurriedly shrugged off her clothes. Watching her, Don Luis' mood mellowed. Her high-breasted young body with its smooth tanned skin had not yet failed to arouse him. Rosalia slipped into bed beside the old man.

'You are a very considerate daughter,' he said, drawing himself onto her warmth. He moved his fingers over her body, seeking the core of her warmth. He found it between her legs. He gnawed hungrily at her breast.

Rosalia stared at the ceiling as the old man thrust into her. The thought of escape was so exciting that tonight she did not have to fake her moans of pleasure.

CHAPTER TEN

Sloane rode towards El Muerte's camp through a sweltering wilderness of sand and wind-chewed rock. He knew the bandits' camp had to be near and that El Muerte would have guards posted along the trail. With luck he'd see the guards before they saw him.

He was out of luck. Two mounted men converged on him from behind rocks on either side of the trail, their grinning teeth bright in dark faces.

'*Buenas Tardes*, Boss,' one of them called out cheerfully as if unaware that he was pointing a rifle at Sloane's chest.

'Howdy,' said Sloane, equally cheerful, as if he hadn't noticed the rifle either.

'What are you doing out here, Boss,' the bandit asked. 'Don't you know this place is dangerous – that it is full of bandits who hate gringos?'

The other bandit chuckled appreciatively.

'I'm looking for a friend of mine,' said Sloane.

'What does he look like your friend, Boss? Maybe we have seen him.'

'He's a priest. He was headed this way in a wagon.'

'Oh, *si*,' the bandit with the rifle grinned. 'He was very brave to come out here all alone that priest. He sure had a lot of balls!'

'*Had?*' Sloane repeated. 'Is he dead?'

'No, Boss, but he sure as hell wishes he was!'

The two bandits laughed. They laughed so much they clutched at their sides.

'That's too bad,' said Sloane mildly.

When he'd wiped the tears of laughter from his face the bandit with the rifle started to get interested in Sloane's saddle-bags. 'What you got in there, Boss – gold?'

'No gold,' said Sloane.

'How 'bout that rifle-case – you got a nice shiny new rifle in there? Maybe a Winchester?'

'Why don't you have a look and see?' Sloane invited him.

The bandit rode closer, keeping his rifle centred on Sloane. 'Open it up, Boss,' he ordered. 'But slow, I got a quick finger . . .'

Sloane opened the rifle-case.

'Show me what you got in there,' the bandit told him.

Sloane obliged him. He pulled the razor-edged sword from the case in an upwards flashing arc. Suddenly the bandit was only half the man he had been. His rifle clattered to the ground. Half of him followed. The lower part of his body remained seated in the saddle, held in place by the *tapaderos* on his feet.

Without a glance at the body Sloane urged the Morgan straight at the other bandit, his dripping blade lifted to kill again. The bandit howled with terror at the sight of the crazed gringo rushing straight at him with a bloody sword. He shrieked in terror, wheeled his pony and rode out, hell-for-leather. Sloane gave chase, holding the reins of his horse in one hand, the raised sword in the other. He could have drawn his Colt and blasted the Mex off his pony but he knew a shot might draw some unwelcome attention.

The two men thundered across the desert, one after the other, raising a cloud of dust. The bandit knew the terrain. He fled down twisting rock-strewn ravines, lashing his galloping pony with the reins. But he couldn't shake off his relentless pursuer. Sloane slowly gained on him.

Glancing constantly back over his shoulder, the bandit saw that Sloane was almost on him, sword hauled back to strike. In desperation he drew a machete from its sheath and, turning in the saddle, hacked frantically at the American.

Sloane parried the blow and the downward slash of his

113

sword sheared through the bandit's shoulder, cleaving his breast-bone. The bandit toppled from the saddle. Sloane reined in, the Morgan rearing. It was then that he noticed that he had company. All around him Mexicans were leaping up like they'd sprung right out of the ground. Most of them had guns and they were pointing them in his direction. Shouting and gesticulating, the mob of angry Mexicans closed on him in a tightening circle. He'd ridden right into a crawling nest of bandits.

Sloane cussed and raised the sword, ready to take a few of them with him before they shot him down. But then a voice called out hastily in Spanish and the seething mob of bandits grew respectfully silent as a tall man dressed completely in black shoved through them towards Sloane.

'Señor Sloane, I was not expecting you so soon,' said the man in black, with a parody of a welcoming smile. His face was gaunt as a part-fleshed skull and the wildness of the desert was in his eyes.

Sloane knew he was looking at the man responsible for killing Chang Fung and Hsiao Yu and maybe a few hundred other people besides.

El Muerte.

Carlos was surprised when he unlocked the door and found Rosalia standing there holding the plate of *tortillas* for Su Fan.

'Chiquita burnt her hand,' Rosalia explained.

Carlos grunted and moved aside for her to enter. He exchanged a sly grin with Pedro, the other guard. It was not often they were honoured by a visit from Don Luis' favourite daughter. Su Fan lay despondently on the bed. She did not bother to look up at Rosalia when she laid the plate down on the table beside the bed. Rosalia looked her over as she might a new riding pony.

'I wanted to see what a yellow woman looks like,' she con-

114

fided in the two guards. 'She doesn't look like much to me. Do you get any fun out of her?' The two guards stared at Rosalia, startled by the leering insinuation from the lips of a girl who looked as pure as the Holy Virgin herself.

'She is too fierce,' Pedro volunteered. 'She has a kick like a mule.'

Rosalia glanced scornfully at the Chinese girl. 'She should be proud to give herself to a pair of good strong Mexican men,' she said, turning her attention back to the two guards. She looked at them in a way that said she liked what she saw. She smiled an inviting smile.

'You look like men who could scratch this itch I have,' she said. 'Don Luis has tried but that little finger of his cannot reach this big itch of mine . . .'

As she spoke Rosalia raised her long skirt up above her thighs. Beneath the skirt she was naked.

'*Por Dios!*' Carlos croaked.

The eyes of the two guards were bugging out of their heads, glued to the dark triangle of silky curls at the junction of her soft thighs. Carlos and Pedro shuffled towards her like starving men drawn forward by the rich aroma of savoury food. Neither of them saw Billy Wang slip into the room through the open door behind them. They never even noticed him until Billy chopped his hand against the back of Pedro's neck. Then it was too late for Pedro to notice anything. He was dead before he touched the ground.

Barking an oath, Carlos whirled round, raising his Sharps rifle to blast the Chinaman. Billy's foot slammed into him and the rifle fell from broken fingers. Carlos doubled up, clutching his shattered hand, howling his pain. Billy's knee rose up in an elephant kick that caught Carlos under the chin and nearly tore his head from his neck. He fell back and sprawled across the floor, blank-eyed.

Su Fan had jumped up from the bed during the brief fight. She stood with her back to the wall, one hand pressed against her mouth. She stared fearfully at Billy, cried out when he pushed past Rosalia and moved quickly towards her. He caught one of her wrists in a powerful grip.

'No!' she cried, struggling to break free.

Billy clamped his other hand over her mouth. He put his face close to hers, a warning in his eyes. 'We're here to help you,' said Billy. 'We're gonna get you out of here!'

Su Fan continued to struggle, shaking her head from side to side.

'Hurry up!' Rosalia hissed urgently from the door where she was keeping an eye on the stairs.

Billy slapped Su Fan across the face, hard. Stunned, she stopped struggling for a moment.

'If you don't come with us – they'll kill you!' he told her. '*Understand?*'

Something in his eyes told her it was useless to struggle any more. She nodded weakly.

Billy took his hand from her mouth and pushed her towards the door.

'Come on, let's go!'

'So you are the gringo who laughs at guns and fights with his hands and feet . . .?'

El Muerte smiled a taunting smile at the lean hard-faced American who stood before him trying to look as if he was unaware of the half-dozen rifles poking into his back.

'I have heard of you, Señor Sloane, of how you killed Pancho Gonzalez.'

The eyes of El Muerte blazed like flaming jewels set in the narrow slits of a mask of beaten gold. Sloane met the burning gaze evenly. His face betrayed no emotion as he stared back into the face of the man he had promised to kill. He thought of Hsiao Yu, of Chang Fung's mutilated body, of Joe and of the nameless tortured victims he had seen on the long trail into Mexico. He thought of the pain in their faces

116

and he wanted to reach out and crush the bandit's neck and feel his body dying beneath his bare hands.

Instead he forced his lips into a smile. 'You another of Pancho's cousins?' he asked.

The bandit laughed and slowly shook his head, the golden earring dancing bright beneath his ear. 'No, señor, I am not. This Pancho called himself a bandit ... but he was a little bandit – little like a bug. He meant nothing to me.'

The bandit's mouth went on smiling but the smile in his eyes went out like a candle flame in a sudden wind. He glared suspiciously at Sloane.

'Only a foolish man would come riding alone into the land of death,' he said. 'You do not look to me like a foolish man, señor ...'

'I'm a tourist,' said Sloane, 'come to take in the sights ...'

'A tourist ... who cuts up my men like pieces of meat on a plate?'

'They were annoying me,' said Sloane.

El Muerte looked like he was trying to make up his mind whether to snarl or smile. The smile struggled through and became a laugh. His laughter broke the tension in the camp. The hostile faces of the bandits crowding round loosened into slack-mouthed grins.

El Muerte gestured towards his men. 'They annoy me too these stinking goats. It is not easy to find good *bandidos* any more ...'

The grins in the faces of the bandits grew even broader.

'You know something, Sloane,' said El Muerte, 'I think perhaps I like you. You are my kind of *hombre*.'

'Well, thanks,' said Sloane. 'That makes me feel real good.'

'I like you so much,' El Muerte continued, 'that I may not kill you until tomorrow ... Tomorrow is a great day – the Day of the Dead!'

'Happy birthday,' said Sloane.

El Muerte laughed some more. Then he shouted an order in Spanish and waved impatiently for his men to disperse. The bandits stopped trying to dig holes in Sloane's back with their rifles and moved away in groups, chattering beneath sombreros. They'd relieved Sloane of his sword and pistol. He lowered his arms and took a look around the camp.

El Muerte's men were settling down to what they'd been doing before Sloane disturbed their peace – eating, drinking, smoking, cleaning their guns and machetes. There were about forty bandits in the camp, Sloane estimated, including some women. The women were as coarse-faced as the rest and except for their skirts, most of them were dressed the same as their men. Beyond the fires around which the bandits squatted Sloane spotted a buckboard. There was a coffin in the back of the buckboard.

'You want to see some sights ... Come, I will show you one,' said El Muerte.

The bandit's spurs made a sound like rattling chains as he walked. Sloane followed him through the camp. Above, a flag hung from a pole, limp in the windless air. The flag was black with a white skull grinning above a pair of crossed bones. El Muerte saw Sloane looking up.

'That was the flag of my ship,' he told him. 'I loved the sea but I love my country more.'

'This why you came back – to become a bandit?'

'In Mexico a poor man has only three choices if he does not want to starve,' El Muerte explained. 'He can become a soldier, a priest or a bandit. A soldier answers to his general and a general answers to the president. A priest has to answer to God ... But a bandit answers to no one but himself.'

'Depends how fast he can run,' Sloane observed.

El Muerte led him to the back of the camp. A circle of

brown-eyed women with bandoliers crossing their chests were busily slapping *tortillas* into shape on the bare earth. Another, with a child clamped to her naked breast, was stirring a bubbling pot of stew which smelled of goat.

'This is how we treat our uninvited guests,' said El Muerte, pointing.

Behind the women, a huge cactus raised its spiky limbs towards the sky. Impaled on the spikes, his arms stretched out, was a naked man. The bandits had had their usual fun with him. The man was no longer a man. It wasn't easy but Sloane recognised Father Josef. There was hardly a part of his body that was not caked with dried blood. Amazingly, the young priest still lived.

El Muerte watched Sloane's face for a reaction. He was disappointed because there wasn't one. The American's face was as impassive as his own.

'Play the saviour and you end up crucified,' said Sloane, turning away.

'I know this saying, it is a good one,' the bandit agreed. 'But perhaps now you think El Muerte is a cruel man?'

'Whatever gave you that idea?' Sloane asked, his smile wry.

'If I am cruel it is because the spirit of my country is in my veins and it is a cruel spirit . . .' El Muerte looked out into the desert, narrowing his eyes against its bone-white glare.

'Out there is hunger, thirst, sickness, death . . . The sting of the scorpion. The claws of the jaguar. A hundred kinds of death for a man to face. In Mexico only vultures get fat, Señor Sloane. Vultures and presidents . . . If I have my sting and my claws, if I kill those that do not please, does that make me any more cruel than the sun that burns or the dry earth that starves? I do not think so.'

Sloane silently contemplated El Muerte. He hated the bandit who had killed Chang Fung and Hsiao Yu – who had stolen Su Fan. He hated him with a fierce burning hatred

119

that only revenge would satisfy. Yet at the same time he felt an affinity with the one who called himself El Muerte, a grudging respect for him. He remembered one of Chang Fung's Chinese sayings –

> 'Heaven and earth are ruthless
> and treat the beasts like straw dogs.
> The wise man is ruthless
> and treats other men like straw dogs . . .'

The Way of the Ruthless Man was the most difficult path of all for a man to take. Chang Fung had warned Sloane against it. He'd said that to be ruthless was the way of the gods not of man – and the gods were fiercely jealous. It was difficult for a man who took the ruthless way to maintain the delicate balance of *Yin* and *Yang* necessary for success in all things. The Ruthless Man needed great merits to balance his ruthlessness, to maintain the precarious balance of negative and positive. Loss of balance meant destruction. Sloane saw in El Muerte a fellow traveller along the way of the Ruthless Man. One who had lost his balance, who had strayed far from the centre.

There was another saying Chang Fung had taught Sloane –

'For him who sees only Death, there is no harmony.'

'That is a very prickly cactus, Señor Sloane,' said El Muerte, turning from the desert back to the dying priest. 'Perhaps now you will tell me why you are here?'

'I heard you had something worth looking at.'

El Muerte watched him, waiting.

'The skull,' said Sloane.

The bandit chief chuckled. 'So you wish to see the Holy Skull.'

'Seein's believing,' said Sloane.

'Very well, I would not want to deprive a man of his last wish . . .'

The bandit led Sloane to a shack made from the spines of dried-up *cadrons*. Inside, a solid wooden sea-chest squatted on a bright-coloured carpet beside a foul litter of clothes, gold pesos, jewels and chewed bones. Sloane watched El Muerte unlock the sea-chest, ignoring the young girl chained up inside the shack.

From the chest El Muerte drew out a compact bundle wrapped in black velvet. He unravelled the bundle and held up its contents for Sloane to see. For the second time that day Sloane looked into the naked face of death.

The sun-glare leaking into the shack made rainbows in the hollow sockets of the crystal skull. Its teeth stretching in an eternal grin, the skull leered at Sloane. Tiny veins seemed to dance redly beneath its crystal skin. A superstitious man would have thought that the Holy Skull glowed with a life of its own. Sloane was not superstitious but he felt the skull's power throbbing, flowing out towards him. Don Luis had been right when he said the skull was more a thing of the Devil than of God.

El Muerte held the skull worshipfully, its face close to his own. 'Do you know why he grins, Sloane?'

'Tell me.'

'It is because he knows that one day when we are dead and eaten by worms, we shall all look like him.'

The bandit looked into the fathomless glowing pits that were the skull's eyes with the same affection as a man looks into the face of his lover.

'Those foolish priests think the skull belongs to their god,' El Muerte laughed. 'They think men of their faith brought the skull to Mexico. They are wrong. This skull was here *mil mil* years before the white men came to steal the gold from our pockets and the smiles from our faces. It was made by my people when they were Kings of the Earth, the Masters of the Sun . . .'

El Muerte raised the skull, putting the fleshless mouth to

his ear as if to catch its dry whisper. 'The ghosts of my people are alive,' said the bandit, his eyes bright as the sun-fired crystal he was holding. 'They live in this skull. Sometimes they speak to me through the mouth of the skull. They tell me what to do, who to kill. Once Don Luis told me these things but now it is the skull. He speaks to me of you, Sloane. He tells me that you are dangerous to me – that you too must die!'

Sloane coolly contemplated the madman that stood before him. 'That talkin' skull must be good comp'ny for you. You'll sure miss it when it's gone.'

Alarm fractured the bandit's blazing eyes. 'What do you mean – when it is *gone*?'

'I'm taking the skull,' said Sloane. 'I'm taking it back to the mission.'

El Muerte stared at Sloane, his alarm softening into amusement.

'Just like that,' he laughed. 'You do not even offer something in exchange!'

'I'm lettin' you have somethin' in exchange,' Sloane told him.

El Muerte waited.

'Your life,' said Sloane. 'I came to kill you. Give me the skull and I'll let you live.'

El Muerte shook his head incredulously. 'You dare threaten me – in my own camp!'

'You're gonna have to give me the skull or kill me,' said Sloane. 'If you set your dogs on me, they'll know you're scared. You want me dead – you're gonna have to do it yourself.'

The bandit thought about it. He lowered his eyes to the skull looking for an answer. He found one and suddenly his grin matched that of the skull.

'You and me, Sloane,' he decided. 'We will dance the

Dance of the Scorpions . . . The one who dances best gets the skull. And the other – the coffin!'

Inside the circle of silently watching bandits, Sloane and El Muerte faced each other. The only sound was the rattle and jangle of El Muerte's razor-sharp spurs as the bandit confidently closed the distance between him and Sloane.

El Muerto opened his attack with a kick at Sloane's groin, the spurs slashing at his manhood. Sloane blocked the kick with his arm in a swift whipping-branch action. At the exact same time, since this was a Scorpion Dance and Sloane was eager to show he was no wall-flower, he backfisted the bandit's face with a scorpion blow.

It was a long time since anyone had knocked El Muerte to the ground. It was almost a new experience for him. But in the next few minutes, it became a regular habit. The bandit wiped sweat from his face onto his sleeve. He looked at the sleeve. His sweat was red. Already he was covered in gashes and bruises. And his lovingly sharpened spurs had yet to sink their teeth into Sloane.

El Muerte attacked again. This time he leapt high into the air as he had seen the yellow men do in distant lands. His spurs flashed towards Sloane's face. This was how El Muerte had blinded Juan and many others before him. The technique had never failed him.

Until now.

Stepping nimbly back, Sloane caught the booted foot at the limit of its kick and pulled – slamming its owner to the ground with bone-rattling impact. Arms folded, he impassively watched the shaken bandit struggle to his feet.

That had been a mistake, El Muerte groggily decided. A mistake that could happen only once. Again he leapt up, a spurred foot slicing through the air at the American's face.

Sloane leapt higher. His flying kick slammed into the bandit's jaw, a head-snapping blow that sent El Muerte spinning backwards through the air a couple of times before he rammed the hard-baked earth with his head. Sloane landed on his feet, neat as a ballet dancer, and watched the stunned killer with satisfaction.

Staggering upright, El Muerte shook his brains back into place. There was fear in his face now – a fear he did not want his shocked silent men to see. His famous spurs had failed him. The situation called for desperate measures. There was a cutlass swinging from El Muerte's studded belt. He tugged it free of its sheath. Swinging it above his head, pirate-fashion, he charged.

A ram's-head fist greeted him. Closely followed by a snap-kick equally eager to make his acquaintance. El Muerte sprawled on the ground, still clutching his cutlass. Sloane was vaguely aware there was something strange about the cutlass but he didn't have time to dwell on its strangeness because pretty soon the bandit was back on his feet, a terrible look on his face as he launched himself with renewed ferocity at the infuriating American.

He hacked and he slashed. The sun-flashing cutlass carved the air. That was all it carved. Wherever the cutlass was, Sloane wasn't. He danced from the sweep of its blade, a smile on his face which El Muerte found more painful than the kicks that battered his body. The bandit gave up the chase. He stood his ground, a defeated expression on his face as he levelled the cutlass in Sloane's direction.

Then Sloane knew what was strange about that cutlass. From behind the blade, a black hole stared at him: the muzzle of a pistol. The Elgin Cutlass gun barked shatteringly when El Muerte pulled the trigger. Sloane spun back, hit the dirt and lay completely still, blood spilling from his head.

Their eyes restless for pursuit, Billy, Rosalia and the Chinese girl they had just helped escape, moved hurriedly towards the ready-saddled horses. Billy pushed Su Fan forward before him like a reluctant prisoner. She flinched at his touch.

'I thought she was your woman,' said Rosalia.

'She is,' Billy snapped from between bared teeth. 'She just doesn't know it yet.'

They reached the horses and thanked their various gods that they had not been seen.

Their gratitude was premature. A group of men ran out from inside the stable and surrounded them, rifles and pistols pointing inwards. Billy snapped out a kick and suddenly there was one less man surrounding them. A *vaquero* lay on the ground with his head at a new angle. It wasn't much of an improvement because he was dead.

His rigid hands tensed hard as knives, Billy took up a defensive position.

'Do not be foolish,' Aguilar warned, aiming a gun. 'Or all three of you die now, the girls first . . .'

Billy looked around. There wasn't much to see but guns. He shrugged defeatedly and lowered his arms. Instantly Toro sprang forward and slubbed him to the ground with the butt of his rifle. He stood over the Chinaman with the rifle raised for further blows, looking to Don Luis for his orders.

'Tomorrow is the Day of the Dead,' said Don Luis. 'His death will liven up the *fiesta*.'

'It should be interesting to see the colour of a Chinaman's blood,' said Aguilar with enthusiasm.

'Kiss my yellow ass!' said Billy.

Toro struck downwards with the rifle-butt and knocked him unconscious.

Don Luis stepped delicately over the Chinaman towards Rosalia. She cowered before him. He reached out and took hold of her dress by the collar. With a savage jerk, he ripped the dress open, baring her breasts.

'*Really*, Papa,' said Rosalia, disgust giving her strength.

125

Don Luis' smouldering anger flared. He cuffed her face and breasts many times. She refused to cry.

'Aguilar, she is yours,' said Don Luis. 'When every man on the ranch has finished with her – *burn* her!'

'*Muchas gracias, patron.*'

Aguilar whitely smiled his thanks.

'Sounds like a damn waste a' good woman flesh to me,' boomed a wide-shouldered black-bearded American, one of several gringos in the group.

'She must be *punished*, Señor Sullivan,' said Don Luis in a voice that suggested further discussion of the matter would be unwelcome. 'But you may have this one as I promised.'

He gestured towards Su Fan. The Chinese girl fearfully returned his stare.

Sullivan looked her over, nodding his approval. 'She'll fetch a good price in 'Frisco,' he predicted. 'There's rich chinkees there desperate for women a' their kind.'

They push-pulled Su Fan over towards a big conestoga wagon. A dozen dark barefoot girls were already cramped inside the wagon, their expressions blank or frightened.

'What beauties!' Aguilar exclaimed, his enthusiasm forced. 'And all pure – all virgins!'

'In a pig's eye!' Sullivan cussed. 'You could run a railroad through some a' them virgins a' yours.'

They heaved Su Fan into the wagon. She sunk down inside, her head bowed, hopelessness overwhelming her. Sloane had never seemed so remote as at that moment.

Sloane lay still as death on the ground, blood flowing from his temple. He hadn't been lying there longer than two blinks when there was a bandit astride him, pressing a stiletto to his throat. The bandit felt for a heartbeat and found one.

'He's alive,' the bandit yelled to El Muerte who was blowing smoke from the shooting-end of the Elgin gun and striking a heroic pose like he was a sharpshooter in a Buffalo Bill Wild West Show.

'Shall I—?'

The tip of the knife pricked deeper into Sloane's throat. Returning the cutlass gun to its sheath, El Muerte strode over to where the eager bandit was squatting atop Sloane's chest. He booted him off the American then looked with respect at the motionless figure in the dust.

'This was a man,' he told the bandit whose name was Miguel. 'A worm does not kill a man.'

Many more bandits were now clustered around Sloane, straining their necks to get a better look at the gringo who had come close to making a dead man out of El Muerte. They nudged the unconscious American with their boots.

'But worms can eat a man!' El Muerte announced with sudden inspiration. He pointed towards the buckboard which had delivered Father Josef to his lingering death.

'Put him in the coffin ... Miguel, take him to the graveyard and bury him with honour. Rico can go with you. Bury him deep so the worms will not have far to look for their dinner!'

Within a short time the coffin intended for Pascual had an unexpected tenant – Sloane. The coffin bounced in the back of the buckboard as Miguel and Rico followed the rutted trail into Lascara. The two bandits talked of profound things. Like Maria the village whore.

'A very deep woman,' said Rico.

'Very,' Miguel agreed.

'Deep as a well,' said Rico.

'But which of us will dip his bucket into this deep well – you or me?'

'Maria has enough love in her heart for both of us,' said Rico. 'She has a big heart.'

'It is not her big heart which interests me,' said Miguel.

Presently, the buckboard rumbled into the graveyard.

Around them wooden crosses grew thick as grass. The grave-yard at Lascara was the most densely populated area of Baja. The reason for its popularity was El Muerte.

Miguel brought the wagon to a halt beside a likely-looking spot for a grave. The two bandits jumped down and turned to unload the wagon. They stopped in their tracks, aston-ished. From inside the coffin a plume of dark smoke drifted upwards. Miguel and Rico exchanged glances of amazement then stepped curiously closer to the coffin, one on either side of it.

Rico slid back the lid and both men peered hesitantly inside.

Sloane was no longer unconscious. He was smoking a cigar. He looked at the bandits who were looking at him and he winked. Then his scissors kick hit them, a boot smashing into each man's face. They staggered back and dis-appeared from his sight. Sloane climbed out of the coffin and jumped down off the wagon after Rico. He felt weak from loss of blood and his head hurt like blazes and he had no time for pleasantries. He caught Rico's arm as the knife swung to meet him and snapped it like a twig across his rising knee just as his elbow hooked back for a monkey blow that left a dent in the bandit's neck. Rico fell like he'd been shot between the eyes.

Brisk thunderclapping gunfire disturbed the sleep of the dead as Sloane rounded on the remaining bandit. Miguel was the other side of the wagon waving a Colt and firing blind. He was firing blind because the corner of Sloane's heel had caught him in the right eye. One hand was clamped across his face trying to fit the mess crawling down his cheek back into the socket where his eye had been whilst the hand with the gun blasted bullets at the world that gave him pain.

One of the wagon horses screamed and tried to rear up, its flank suddenly wet and red from a stray bullet. The other horse spooked and bolted, dragging the wagon with it. A wheel of the wagon ran up against a tomb-stone and parted company with the chassis. A second later wagon and horses spilled over in a rolling heap of thrusting legs and disintegrating wood.

Miguel had run out of bullets. He threw the empty Colt from him with a snarling cry that was part anger and mostly pain. He never saw Sloane coming at him, never heard him above the ruckus of the screaming horses – but he felt the impact of the flying kick that exploded the air from his lungs and sent him flying backwards, arms grabbing at air. He went on flying back until his head met a headstone. The headstone was harder.

Sloane had landed badly. His wound was bleeding again and he felt dazed as a spinning top. He struggled up, took a few drunken steps, then pitched forward onto his face and lay still.

CHAPTER ELEVEN

It was crowded in the small dark room where Sloane awoke. It was crowded but it was silent as the grave. Sloane looked into the dark faces of his companions. The faces were shrivelled as ancient oranges and as dry-looking as a handful of ashes. The owners of the faces didn't seem very excited to see that Sloane was alive. They didn't make any fuss at all. They lay there with their backs to the wall, still as death. Which wasn't surprising because they'd all been dead for a very long time.

Wrinkling his nose, Sloane tore his eyes from the blankly smiling corpses and took a look around the mummy cave. Further along, the rough uneven stone wall was splashed with light, suggesting an opening that he could not see. When he looked back at his crumbling companions the dark face of one of them had split into a broad gleaming grin.

'If you're Saint Peter, I'm in the wrong place,' said Sloane.

'How you feelin', Missuh Sloane?' Dred Jefferson inquired.

'On top of the world,' said Sloane, then groaned as he tried to sit up straight and a sharp pain axed through his skull.

'Guess I just fell off again,' he added.

Raising a hand he touched his aching forehead. He found his head was bandaged.

'It's just a graze – reckon you'll live,' the bone-devil told him.

'When I seen you lyin' there wi' your head all bloodied up, I reckoned you was stone-dead. Thought I was gonna have me that purty three-dollar head a' your'n f'sure. Then I seen you was still breathin' . . .'

'Real inconsiderate of me,' said Sloane.

'Sure is . . . Holding out like that on a man tryin' to make hisself a decent livin'. Reckon you're owin' me a head, Missuh Sloane.'

'I'll see you get one,' Sloane promised. He flicked his eyes towards the mummies. 'Why'd you bring me here?' he asked.

'Safest place there is. El Muerte'll be riding into Lascara tomorrow for the Day of the Dead – an' he's goin' be madder'n a bee-stung mule when he sees what you done to his men.'

Sloane was silent for a moment, head lowered in thought. When he looked up at the negro, there was a grim determined smile tugging at the corners of his mouth.

'That priest, Father Francesco . . . can you fetch him here?'

'You goin' die?' the bone-devil asked, quick and hopeful.

'Now don't go raisin' your expectations like that,' Sloane told him. 'The padre and me's got some talkin' to do . . . There's some mighty strong stuff down in his wine cellar – stuff as'll make the party go with a bang.'

Dred frowned. '*Party?* What party you talkin' 'bout?'

'The party I'm throwing for El Muerte,' said Sloane, a savage glint of humour in his eyes. 'His birthday party!'

The white globe of heat above had reached its highest point and was beginning its leisurely climb down the sky when El Muerte rode into Lascara to celebrate the Day of the Dead. Behind him rode his men, forty of them in a tight dense herd. Trailed by barking dogs, the bandits thundered down the narrow *calles* of mud huts and small adobes. They were in loud good spirits, their mood already warmed by *tequila* and by thoughts of the pleasures the rest of the day – and night – would bring. El Muerte led them clattering into the small *plaza* at the heart of the village. On market days and *fiestas* the *plaza* was always thronged with people having a good noisy time and by vendors displaying fruits and vegetables in brightly coloured heaps.

Today there wasn't a soul in the *plaza*. The bandits circled and wheeled inside the empty square, eyes searching for signs of life. They grew silent, their boisterous mood chased away by uneasy suspicions.

Usually on feast-days many stalls were set up inside the *plaza* – stalls for *tequila* and *pulque* and wine and candies and goods of many kinds. But today there was only one stall. It was loaded with crisp white candy skulls in all sizes and with little wooden coffins, the kind small boys love to fill with firecrackers. El Muerte peered down at the sugar skulls then swung his black horse round and angrily scanned the deserted streets and lifeless houses.

'Hey, you sons of pigs,' he yelled. 'Where is the *tequila*? Where are the girls? . . . Where are the gifts to honour El Muerte on this very fine Day of the Dead? . . . Come on out quick – or we will come in and drag you from your filthy holes!'

El Muerte waited for results. A couple of stringy dogs barked at him. Otherwise there was silence.

'*Mira!*'

One of his men was pointing. El Muerte followed the direction of the shakily outstretched hand. Propped against a wall were Miguel and Rico, both looking very dead. Between them, also leaning against the wall was a coffin. A thin spiral of smoke drifted skywards from the coffin.

El Muerte glared at the bodies of his two men, and at the smoking coffin. He tugged a heavy calibre pistol from its holster, aimed it at the coffin and squeezed off a rapid succession of shots.

Lascara blew up in his face. The impact of the deafening

explosion hurled men and horses into the air, slamming them against each other and against the remaining walls of the *plaza*. The explosion ripped a chunk out of the square. The house against which the coffin had been leaning was suddenly gone. Only a small pile of rubble showed it had ever existed.

El Muerte raised himself painfully from the ground where he'd been thrown. He felt like someone had landed a terrific punch against his head. He touched his face with his hands and they came away bloody. His face was skinned and peppered with chips of stone. He didn't know Sloane was throwing him a surprise party – but he sure felt surprised.

He crawled to his feet. A dark fog-like curtain of smoke and choking dust boiled around the *plaza*. Pieces of the coffin were burning on the ground. El Muerte heard the screams of men and horses he could not see. And sporadic blasts of gunfire. His own pistol was gone, torn from his hand by the force of the explosion. He slid a machete from his belt and, with the blade held before him, advanced unsteadily through the smoke and dust, searching for his horse.

The dust bit at his lungs. He coughed and clamped his free hand over his mouth. Terrified riderless horses charged blindly through the smoke. He leapt aside to avoid them. One reared at the sight of him and he had to roll beneath its thrusting hooves. Twice he stumbled over bodies. The bodies of many of his men littered the *plaza*. Not enough was left of some of them to be called a body.

Gradually the smoke cleared.

Through the thinning curtain of smoke, El Muerte saw about half his men were on their feet, many of them shocked and dazed. Others were alive but lay groaning where they had fallen, too injured to stand. As if by a miracle a few men had managed to stay in the saddle. Riderless horses were chasing around the *plaza*, kicking and bucking when men made a grab at their trailing reins.

'Get those horses!' El Muerte ordered, his voice a scream.

The bandits chased after the panicked beasts in a scrambling, shouting pack that only panicked them more.

El Muerte's own horse lay on the ground in a panting sweat. One of its legs was broken and the explosion had driven a big sliver of the coffin deep into its flank. El Muerte knelt beside the shuddering animal and gentled it, his voice low and soft. Then, seeing it was hopeless, he slashed the horse's throat with his machete. A hot gush of blood muddied the sand. El Muerte dragged his saddle-bags free of the horse. From inside he took a bundle wrapped in black velvet. The way he clutched the bundle said he'd kill anyone who tried to take it from him.

The sound of galloping horses jerked his head alert. Three of his men were taking off galloping out of the *plaza* down one of the small narrow *calles* leading off from it.

'Come back, you bastards!' he screamed. '*Halto*, you pigs of cowards!'

The bandits paid him no attention. They rode straight out of the *plaza* as fast as their digging spurs could persuade their horses to carry them. A few seconds later the voices of the escaping bandits were heard to rise in shrill agonised screams that died as suddenly as they began. That was all it took to break the already demoralised spirits of El Muerte's men. All who still had horses dug spurs into their flanks and rode wildly towards another of the small *calles*.

'Traitors! Wait for me!' El Muerte shrieked as they galloped past him. He didn't have a horse and he didn't like the idea of being left behind by those who did.

Nearby a pistol lay on the ground where it had fallen from the twitching hand of its dead owner. El Muerte dived for it and came up shooting at the nearest deserter. One of the bullets hit the horse instead. The horse buckled, spilling its rider. The bandit rolled, then scrambled up, one hand tugging at the grip of his pistol. El Muerte fired again. The bullet delivered a soggy punch to the man's face and knocked him flat.

The rest of the escaping horsemen didn't get very much further. They'd ridden half-way down the narrow passage when they discovered the other end was blocked by a barrel large enough to fill the width of the *calle*. The barrel was rolling their way and it looked heavy and there was a fuse sparking at its side.

Suddenly the men on horses were as mad-anxious to get back to the *plaza* as they had been to escape from it a minute before. The bandits jostled frantically to swing their horses round in the narrow *calle*. Horses plunged into each other, shrilling in protest. One bandit flew from the back of his rearing mount. He fell directly in the path of the lumbering barrel. By the time he'd leapt to his feet, the barrel was almost on him. He limped away from it as fast as he could. Which wasn't fast enough. The barrel rolled straight over him, crushing him face-down in the dirt.

The struggling mess of riders had just made it back into the *plaza* when the barrel caught up. It hurtled into the thick of them, ramming horses, snapping their twig legs with its weight.

Then it blew.

When the almighty roar of the blast had died to a hollow growl, Sloane raised his head from the roof-top where he lay and peered down into the *plaza*. The whole square was aboil with smoke and dust which made it impossible to see if anyone had survived the explosion. Then he heard coughing and a near-hysterical voice shouting in rapid-fire Spanish and Sloane smiled a thin smile because he knew El Muerte was still alive. Which meant he could still be killed.

Attached to the heavy buckle of Sloane's belt were three metal stars, each about the size of a sheriff's badge. The stars looked like ornaments which is what they were meant to

135

look like. Sloane plucked one of the stars from his belt, holding the razor-sharp spikes of the *shuriken* with familiar care. Then he heard someone running in the *plaza* below, heading his way.

The running bandit gaped in surprise when the savage-faced gringo in the dirty white suit dropped from the roof directly in his path. He recognised the man he thought was dead and his open mouth started to fill with a scream. But then Sloane's hand flashed out with a heel-of-the-hand blow that drove his nose right back into his brain.

Sloane stepped past the crumpled body and into the rolling mass of smoke. The ground was littered with debris – horse debris and human debris. The bone-devil was going to be cleaning up in more ways than one, Sloane realised and smiled grimly.

He saw the next bandit the same instant the Mex saw him. The bandit threw up his pistol to fire. Then he shrieked and dropped the pistol, one hand clawing at the metal shooting star piercing his eye. He wrenched the star from his head and shrieked louder when his eye came with it.

'I can't abide to see a man sufferin',' said Sloane appearing at his side. Then he did the bandit a merciful favour. He killed him.

Clutching his bundle in one hand and the raised pistol in the other, El Muerte advanced cautiously through the blinding curtain of smoke. The shrieks of pain that speared the silence rattled him. And so did the abrupt way they ended.

'Rafael . . . you still there?' he called.

'*Si, jefecito,*' came the answer, sounding strained and desperate. 'And Jesus and Pacito also . . .'

From the sound of his voice, Rafael and the others were close by, El Muerte decided. But they could as well have been the other side of a mountain so thick was the fog of smoke and dust between him and his few remaining men.

'And Julio?'

'I do not know,' Rafael called back. 'He was here just a moment ago.'

'Julio – are you there?'

No answer.

'*Julio!*'

Silence.

'Is anybody else here?' El Muerte appealed. He could not believe that out of his forty men only three were still alive.

'Just me,' replied a voice that wasn't Julio. An American-sounding voice. Close by.

El Muerte peered into the veil of smoke, straining to catch sight of movement. He raised his pistol higher, earing back the hammer. He knew he had to get the intruder to speak again and betray his position.

'You . . . Who are you?' he urged. 'Don't you got no name?'

'You know who I am . . .'

'Tell me!' El Muerte appealed, aiming his gun into the crowding darkness, finger tightening on trigger.

'The one what's gonna kill you,' the stranger's voice promised.

El Muerte squeezed off two shots in the direction from which the voice came.

He listened. The voice had sounded so familiar. He shook his head. No, it couldn't be, he told himself. But, with a sinking feeling, he knew he was right.

'Better luck next time,' Sloane called sympathetically.

El Muerte gritted his teeth and resisted an angry urge to shoot again. He checked the cylinder of his pistol and confirmed his fear. He only had one shot left. He wasn't going to waste it.

'Rafael . . . Pacito . . . Jesus . . . Don't split up!' he ordered. 'Keep together . . . He is between us. Move towards me and we will catch him in the middle!'

'*Si, jefecito,*' Rafael answered. 'We are coming . . .'

Clutching his precious bundle, pistol ready in his other hand, El Muerte took a cautious step forward into the swirling dust.

Sloane watched the three jittery Mexicans advancing slowly towards him across the dust-whipped *plaza*. He was crouched low, knowing they would be searching for him at eye-level. He let them approach until they were so close he could hear Pacito's teeth chattering. Then he rose swiftly in their path behind a leaping roundhouse kick that instantly shattered Rafael's Winchester into two pieces. The next instant he was amongst them, his hands chopping them down with the effortless ease of a machete hacking through rotten branches.

El Muerte hurried forward at the sound of men fighting. Men fighting and dying . . . That was something he could understand. Something he could come to grips with – not like the taunting voice of a stalking enemy he could not even see. One last choking cry and then the fighting stopped and the uncomfortable silence rushed back to surround El Muerte.

'Rafael?' he called. 'Pacito . . .?'

No answer came. And then El Muerte knew he was alone. There was just him and a man without a face who had promised to kill him.

The dust was settling now and the smoke rapidly fading. Shapes began to separate themselves from the swirl of dust. One of the shapes became a man. El Muerte stood stock-still, his breath held back. He watched the man moving towards him, blind and unsuspecting. He took careful aim at the broad centre of the man. He wanted to make his last bullet count.

He fired. The man grunted and stumbled back, hands grabbing at his belly. Then the man caught his balance and staggered forward once more, moving sluggishly as if struggling against a fierce blizzard. After a few steps he pitched forward onto the ground by El Muerte's feet, a low moan escaping his lips as he died. El Muerte looked down at the dead man. It was Rafael.

The empty gun dropped from El Muerte's fingers. He stared at the body. After a time he raised his eyes and, as he expected, Sloane was before him – a stark grim figure looming phantom-like out of the dust.

'You are either a ghost or a man with a very hard head,' said the bandit. He tossed the bundle he carried lightly to the ground and drew the machete from its sheath.

'If you are a ghost you cannot harm me. If a man . . .'

El Muerte shrugged. Then he charged. He swung the machete in a broad swooping arc aimed at Sloane's neck. Sloane failed to meet the appointment. He side-stepped and the machete sliced empty air, whistling with disappointment. El Muerte tried again, this time slashing low at the American's stomach. Sloane's upthrust knee hammered the bandit's hand and, the same instant, his right hand flashed out in a fast snatching motion.

Springing back out of reach of the machete, Sloane held up his hand – dangling an object for the bandit's benefit. The object was tiny and golden and tinkled sweetly.

El Muerte's earring.

Pain gouging through him, El Muerte clamped a hand to the side of his head and felt the ragged tear in his ear. His eyes bulged furiously in a face that seemed suddenly filled with teeth. Screaming defiance, he pressed his attack, slashing and hacking with frenzied determination. The hissing blade cut patterns in the air. It never touched Sloane. But Sloane's hands and feet touched El Muerte. They touched him and they battered him.

As the two men fought, the villagers of Lascara filed solemnly into the *plaza*. They moved slowly through the dying wisps of smoke, picking their way over the bodies littering the ground. At the head of the procession was Father

Francesco and immediately behind him came El Muerte's victims. Some limped and some hopped on crutches. Those that could see led those who could not.

The Unfortunate Ones of Lascara were the guests of honour at El Muerte's birthday party. They'd each brought a present too. Every one of them gripped a knife or machete or some other kind of sharp cutting blade.

Silently, the grim procession shuffled into the *plaza*, forming a circle around the two men fighting at its centre. A new kind of fear tugged at El Muerte's heart when he saw the villagers surrounding him. He knew what he'd done to them and what they would do to him if they got their hands on him. The knowledge spurred him to attack Sloane with greater ferocity.

It didn't matter how fierce his attack was. Sloane still managed effortlessly to block and counter the strokes of his blade. With growing despair El Muerte realised that the American was playing with him, biding his time for the right moment.

The moment came soon enough. When he saw that all the villagers had taken up their positions in the *plaza*, Sloane knew it was time to end the party-games and get down to the serious business of handing out the presents. As El Muerte lunged at his face with the machete, Sloane's left shot out and caught the upraised wrist in a grip of tightening steel. Then he chopped at the bandit's arm with the hardened edge of his right hand. The arm broke with a sound of dry wood snapping.

The bandit fell back howling. Sloane didn't mind. It was El Muerte's party and he could cry if he wanted. El Muerte's machete fell from pain-stretched fingers. His face was a mask of agony and hatred, the lips peeled back over grinding teeth. But El Muerte was no party-pooper. He wanted the party to go on. Gathering his strength, he ran forward and kicked high, the heel and spurs of his boot leaping up at Sloane's face.

Sloane dodged the raking spurs. Simultaneously, he caught the booted foot at the height of its kick. His right hand slammed down against the rigidly-held leg and shattered it. In the same fluid motion he snapped his elbow straight and backfisted the bandit's groin.

El Muerte collapsed. His broken body writhed in the dust, jack-knifing in pain.

Sloane stooped and picked up the velvet-wrapped bundle from where El Muerte had dropped it. He looked inside. The crystal skull leered at him with its grin of bare-faced evil. He covered up the skull, returning his attention to the bandit groaning at his feet.

'I came a long way to kill you, Mister El Muerte,' he said, 'but I guess these people got their claim staked first.'

Sloane turned to face the watching villagers. 'He's all yours,' he said. 'If you want him – come and get him!'

They didn't need further persuading. The ranks of villagers closed round the bandit chief, all anxious to offer him their congratulations on the Day of the Dead.

El Muerte tried to crawl away. But he was slow and the villagers were eager and fast. When the terrible screams began, Father Francesco averted his head, his lips mouthing prayers.

'*Yo soy la Muerte!*' the bandit screamed. 'You cannot kill Death. You cannot kill *me!*'

The villagers weren't convinced. But just to make sure they kept their blades busy until long after El Muerte quit his squirming and screaming.

CHAPTER TWELVE

Sloane swung down from the big pinto the villagers had given him and dallied the reins round a low branch. He looked up. From where he stood, he could see the fierce glow of a blazing fire over by Don Luis' *hacienda*. He sat down, leaning his back against the trunk of a sweet-smelling *jacaranda*. His head and body ached and he felt very weary. He closed his eyes.

For a long time he sat there in the same position, unmoving except for the regular ebb and swell of his breath. Gradually, mind and body relaxed. Soon he felt the *Tch'i*, his inner strength, flowing through him, filling his body with power and energy. He would need all the power his inner strength could give him in the battle ahead. Sloane had destroyed El Muerte. But he knew El Muerte had been like a deadly fist carrying out instructions received from the brain. Now he had to destroy the brain that guided the fist.

When he felt ready, he opened his eyes and stood. He snapped into a rapid series of exercises, limbering his muscles. Then he headed for the *hacienda*. Carrying a bundle wrapped in black velvet.

He made it unseen to the *hacienda*. He was close enough now to hear the crackle of the big leaping fire in the grounds of the *hacienda*. Men's laughter came from the direction of the fire. Head bent low, Sloane crept closer to the flames. They'd built the fire near the same spot where he had fought Toro. He took cover behind the big cannon that overlooked the scene. He peered over the top of the cold black barrel.

More than twenty *vaqueros* were gathered around the fire, smoking and laughing and loudly celebrating the Day of the Dead. It looked like they were going to have themselves a barbecue. Sloane didn't need to be told who was going to get barbecued. A short distance from the *vaqueros* sat Billy. He was trussed up like a Thanksgiving turkey.

Sloane scanned the faces caught in the glare of the fire. He couldn't see Aguilar or Toro. Or Don Luis. After a time, Sloane moved silently away from the cannon and slid back into the darkness beyond the fire. He was no longer carrying the velvet-wrapped bundle.

Joe had spoken true of his horse. It was the goldenest palamino Sloane had ever clapped eyes on. Its mane and the thick mass of tail-hair were snow-white – but the rest of its sleek body was as bright golden as a bullion bar in the sun. The horse snorted and restlessly shifted as Sloane looked it over.

'Easy, boy, easy . . .' he coaxed and reached across the rails to gentle the animal. But his scent was unfamiliar. The palamino tossed its head to one side and moved back stiff-legged with a low, restless whinny. Its unease spread to the other horses penned in the corral and soon all of them were snorting and stamping.

'*Qué passa, caballos?*'

Sloane ducked behind the corral as a *vaquero* clutching a carbine hurried over to investigate the disturbance.

'*Sta bueno,*' the guard told the shuffling horses to reassure them. Then, to reassure himself, he began a slow sharp-eyed prowl of the perimeter of the corral.

Sloane rose suddenly before him, his foot swinging up for an under-the-chin kick that lifted the Mexican's heels off the ground. The Mex flew back, his head chasing his hat and the rest of his body coming along for the ride. He landed in a heap, his neck at a crazy angle.

The brief flurry of violence made the horses jumpier than ever. They roamed from one end of the corral to the other, heads nodding with growing impatience. Sloane stripped the guard's poncho from his body and struggled into it himself. Then he tugged the body over to the corral and heaved it into a water trough, water spilling over the sides. He pushed the body beneath the water and held it down until it stayed under the surface without his help. He untied the corral gate and held it open.

The horses were suspicious at first. Then they got the idea and there was no holding them back. They pressed eagerly forward, bunching up, squeezing out of the gate one at a time. In less than two minutes, the corral was empty.

Sloane paused briefly to watch the horses thundering away, the flying-maned palamino leading them under the moon. Then he snatched the guard's leather hat from the ground, clamped it on his head and ran into the darkness as the cries of alarm and running footsteps grew rapidly louder.

From the cover of a barn, Sloane watched the *vaqueros* race over to the empty corral, drawn from their fire by the noise of the stampeding horses. They ganged up alongside the corral, all waving their arms and shouting at once. Pretty soon Aguilar ran up and joined them and he shouted louder than all the rest of them. Whatever it was he shouted sent the *vaqueros* scooting towards the stables. There were more horses in the stables and moments later the *vaqueros* rode out in pursuit, lashing at their mounts with quirts. Sloane allowed himself a smile. The escaping horses would be in Alaska before the *vaqueros* caught up with them.

Aguilar was left alone by the corral. He watched the horsemen recede into the night, then turned and headed back towards the *hacienda*, shaking his head. Sloane walked towards him, the wide leather hat tugged low over his face.

When Aguilar saw the man in the rainbow poncho approaching, he stopped and yelled something Spanish in an angry voice. The man in the poncho kept on coming. Aguilar yelled louder and angrier. The man came steadily nearer.

144

Aguilar's hand flew to the butt of his pistol. He had the pistol half out of its holster when something struck his hand with such violent force that the gun was torn from his grasp. He thought a bullet had hit him. Then he remembered he hadn't heard a shot.

Sloane followed up the lightning kick with an inverted fist strike to the head. Aguilar sprawled backwards, twisting as he fell. Sloane helped him on his way with a snap-kick in the ass.

When he'd got tired of lying with his nose pressed into the dust, Aguilar groggily palmed himself up onto his knees. Sloane was waiting for him. He curled his left arm round the Mexican's neck, tight as a noose. He kept him doubled-up at waist level.

Aguilar squirmed in the iron grip but he couldn't break it. Twisting his head round, he succeeded in getting a look at the man who held him.

'*You!*' He sounded surprised and disgusted at the same time.

'Sure looks that way, don't it,' said Sloane.

'Please, señor . . . unhand me. Let me go . . .'

'Now don't tell me you want to leave already – just when we were gonna have ourselves a nice quiet little talk . . .'

'Talk?' Aguilar asked weakly.

'Sure, I know all you Mexicans love to talk. You talk and I'll listen . . . First you tell me who killed the girl's folks – the old Chinaman and his wife . . .'

Suddenly, Aguilar's eyes were wide-stretched and fearful-looking. 'You are mistaken, señor, I –'

'You had Joe killed,' Sloane patiently reminded him. 'You had him killed when you heard he'd gotten a look at El Muerte's gang and you were afraid he'd remember you an' Toro. Because you two were with El Muerte when he went raidin' across the border . . .'

'You're mad!' Aguilar laughed. It was a desperate-sounding laugh.

'Damn right I'm mad,' said Sloane. 'I'm mad as Hell and I'm gonna take it out on you!'

Sloane's knee slammed into Aguilar's face. Six times. Aguilar spluttered, his mouth full of blood.

'Now you tell me who killed 'em . . . Tell me and maybe I'll let you crawl out of here whilst you still got a face.'

'Go to Hell!' Aguilar spat.

Sloane's knee hammered him again. Blood dripped steadily from Aguilar's nose and mouth and beaded the dust.

'Talk some more,' said Sloane. 'I like the sound of your voice.'

'I spit on your mother's grave!'

'You're just bashful,' said Sloane. 'What you need is some encouragement . . .'

Sloane's knee did some encouraging. It was very persuasive encouragement. Soon Aguilar was talking like he had jawbone diarrhoea.

'It was Toro killed the Chinaman,' he said. 'I do not know who killed the woman . . .'

He tried to raise his head. He couldn't.

'Señor, believe me . . . I never wanted to go with that madman . . . Don Luis ordered us!'

'How 'bout the girl?' Sloane asked. 'She all right?'

Suddenly, Aguilar seemed to have lost his urge to talk.

'*The girl* . . .' Sloan repeated, applying pressure.

Aguilar grunted with pain. 'Sullivan took her,' he sullenly revealed.

Sloane gripped the Mexican's head tighter. He almost jerked it from his neck.

'Who the Hell is Sullivan?' he demanded.

Aguilar couldn't answer. He was struggling for breath. Sloane relaxed his grip obligingly.

'An Americano,' Aguilar gasped when he could. 'Don

Luis gives to him girls – in exchange for guns . . . for the revolution.'

'Where'd he take her?'

'They left yesterday – for San Francisco.'

'Hell!' said Sloane.

Then he let Aguilar drop. The Mexican slumped heavily to the ground.

'If I see you again – I'll kill you!' Sloane promised him. He turned on his heel, moving away. When he'd taken three steps, he pivoted suddenly, his roundhouse kick swiping the the knife from Aguilar's hand. Before even his feet touched the ground, two stabbing fingers had buried themselves in the softness of Aguilar's throat. Impaled on the deep-thrust fingers, Aguilar swayed, staring at Sloane with horrified surprise. He made choking sounds, liquid breaths gushing from his mouth. Then Sloane jerked his fingers free and Aguilar fell, his face slopping down into his own blood.

Sloane turned once more and continued on his way.

They'd left an ageing *vaquero* to stand guard over Billy. The guard was heaping wood on the fire to keep it ablaze when he noticed the man in the rainbow poncho approaching. He recognised the poncho. It belonged to a good friend of his.

'*Hola, muchacho!*' he called out cordially.

Sloane strolled up to the guard and, without a word, chopped a hand at his temple. The *vaquero* fell dead. Sloane threw the leather hat into the fire and the poncho followed a moment later.

'I'm sure glad to see you,' said Billy with relief.

The dead guard had a machete at his waist. Sloane slid it from its sheath and slashed through the ropes binding the young Chinaman.

'Things gettin' a bit hot for you round here?' he asked.

'Hot enough. They were fixing to stick me on that fire and roast me.'

'Nice people,' said Sloane.

Billy flexed his arms to get the circulation going. His pleasure at being released was quickly over. He looked downcast.

'Su Fan's gone,' he said. 'A guy called Sullivan –'

'I know,' said Sloane.

He took hold of Billy's arm and led him from the fire. He pointed into the distance where the vague forms of trees reared darker against the sky than the blue of night.

'Over among them trees, you'll find a horse,' he told Billy. 'Take it. They won't have gotten very far in a day. Not in this country.'

Billy searched his face, frowning.

'How about you?' he asked.

Sloane looked narrowly at the Chinaman.

'She's your woman, ain't she?'

Billy shifted his eyes from Sloane's face. He nodded wordlessly.

'Then get after her . . . I got business here needs finishing.'

Sloane turned and walked from him.

'Sloane . . .'

Sloane paused to look back at the Chinaman.

'Did you . . .?' Billy left the question unfinished.

'I got him,' said Sloane.

'I'm glad,' said Billy. And smiled.

Slapping the flat side of the machete against his palm, Sloane headed for the smaller of the two adobe buildings. The one with barred windows.

There was a guard at the top of the stairs. The machete in Sloane's hand went snickety-snick and the guard's head went clumpety-clump as it rolled down the stairs.

At the door, Sloane hesitated, listening to the whimpering

cries of the girl inside – and the coarse laughter of the men with her. For a moment he thought the girl was Su Fan. He thrust the thought aside but the anger remained. He opened the door and entered.

Inside the room, five *vaqueros* stood with their backs to him. None of them spared him a glance because all their attention was on the bed over at the other end of the room.

Toro was on the bed and he wasn't alone. There wasn't much to see of the big Mexican except his big bare ass. It was the fastest moving thing in the room. Toro was doing something to the naked girl pinned beneath his weight. He looked like he was enjoying himself. The girl didn't seem to share his enthusiasm. She was sobbing as she drummed her fists ineffectually against the massive body jammed between her legs. The girl was Rosalia.

Toro was laughing at her struggles as he had his fun. Then, suddenly, he reared his head and howled with pain. Something had bitten into one of the fat white cheeks of his ass. Something sharp . . . A shiny metal star.

Sloane threw another of the *shuriken* as the five Mexicans whirled to meet him. It buried itself in the throat of one of the men, opening up a vein. The man shrieked and fell back, a fierce red spray spouting through his clutching fingers. Into the belly of the nearest Mexican, Sloane buried the machete to the hilt. Then, before the body had even started to fall, he launched himself into the air for a flying swing kick – his foot crunching into the faces of all three men on a single pivot. The *vaqueros* skittled to the floor.

One of them had not learned his lesson. He was still alive and he was trying to aim his gun. Sloane's left foot pounded his gun-hand whilst his right came down in a crushing dragon stamp on the man's chest. Sloane felt the rib-cage collapse beneath his stamping foot.

Then he felt something else – a massive arm winding round his neck with crushing strength. Another pinning his own arms to his side. Sloane thrashed against a merciless grip as Toro lifted him from the ground, pressing a knee into his back, arching his body with a spine-cracking force. The Mexican was slowly breaking him in half!

Sloane kicked strongly backwards. His heel hooked into soft yielding flesh. A groan of pain burst from the big Mexican's lips. He gritted his teeth against the pain, refusing to break the strangle-hold. Again Sloane's foot slammed between his legs. Toro groaned louder. Tears splashed down his cheeks. But with the insane determination of a fanatic, he tightened his grip.

Sloane hammered his foot back a third time into the Mexican's flesh. This time the pain was too much even for Toro. With a roar of agony, he released his hold and Sloane slipped from his grasp. Toro doubled up, clutching his bruised manhood. Sloane pivoted fast and his leaping round-house kick exploded against the side of Toro's thick skull. The blow hurled the Mexican backwards. Sloane leapt after him, battering the big man's chest with a straight-legged flying kick. Toro hurtled back even faster. The wall was waiting for him and the whole room shuddered when they found each other.

Rosalia clapped her hands delightedly. She was huddled on the bed, a blanket not quite covering her nakedness, following the fight with lip-biting attention.

'Give it to him,' she told Sloane as Toro raised himself from the floor. 'Give it to him *good!*'

Toro glared at her. His eyes promised her death when he'd finished with Sloane. He seized a chair from the floor and hurled it at the American.

Sloane chopped the chair out of the air. Toro was right behind it, a low bestial growl rumbling from his throat as he advanced. He made fists of his big-knuckled hands and struck at Sloane, wielding his arms like wooden clubs. Sloane's hands moved with blinding speed, blocking the hail of blows and snapping back dragon-fisted punches. He was weak from loss of blood and knew his punches lacked their usual power. Toro knew it too. He stood his ground, taking all the punishment Sloane could give him. He paid no more attention to the fists that pounded him than if they were raindrops. He knew Sloane was weakening. Sooner or later one of his battering punches would smash through Sloane's defences and open the way for more. Many more. And then he would tear the American apart piece by piece, doing to him what El Muerte's bandits did with their victims. Not with a knife but with his bare hands.

The two men stood there for a long moment, furiously exchanging blows. Soon Toro's nose was twistedly broken and his thick lips torn. His whole face was covered with blood and it rolled down his chest in spiky streams. But his endurance was rewarded. One of his thick-knuckled fists clubbed through the block that met it and hammered the wound at Sloane's temple, gouging it raw.

Sloane staggered, his head blasted by pain. His arms hung limp, his defences briefly forgotten. The Mexican sent a second hammer-headed blow cracking against his head. Sloane dropped, pole-axed. With a growl of pleasure, Toro moved in to boot Sloane's head from his body.

Sloane was down but he wasn't finished. His sweeping kick jerked the Mexican's feet from under him. Toro rubbed cheeks with the floor. Things look different from the floor. You notice things you don't always see from six feet up. Toro noticed something now. The sword Aguilar had left propped against one wall.

Scrambling up, Toro made a dive for the sword. Rosalia saw it too. She scrambled from the bed after it. Toro got there first. He snatched the sword and backhanded Rosalia across the mouth. She fell. Swerving round, Toro saw that Sloane was still lying on the floor, his head wracked with pain. Toro rushed at him, sword raised to strike.

Choking fury chased away the pain in Sloane's head when he saw the Mexican coming at him clutching a sword. Sloane recognised the sword. It belonged to Chang Fung.

Towering over the fallen American, Toro hauled the sword back two-handed over his head for a butchering downward thrust that would cut Sloane in two. Roaring a bull-like bellow of triumph, he struck.

Sloane answered Toro's roar with a savage *ki-ai* yell of his own. The falling sword got no further than the fore-arm block which shattered Toro's arm. The same instant, Sloane's stiff-fingered right flashed out in a knife-hand thrust. The deep-thrust hand sank to the wrist in Toro's solar plexus. When Sloane yanked out his bloodied hand, it was no longer empty.

Voicing a long and terrible scream, Toro staggered back and slammed into a wall. The expression on his face was a fearful one. Rosalia saw it and she squeezed her eyes shut with a trembling shudder.

Toro's eyes and tongue were straining from his head. Then something in his face flickered out and his eyes became opaque. He slid down the wall and lay sprawled in a heap, his life emptying out onto the floor.

Sloane rose to his feet and steadied himself. He took a step forward and looked down without pity at Toro's spasm-jerked body. The Chinese proverb said: *A Man shall not live under the same Heaven as the Murderer of his Father.* Now he could start living again, Sloane thought.

The gods had other ideas. Rosalia's scream warned him when the two men silently entered behind. He whirled round, snapping into a defensive crouch. But fists were no defence against the pistol-shot that nailed him to the ground.

CHAPTER THIRTEEN

The smoking Deringer held delicately in his hand, Don Luis Fernando de Silviera y Castilia stepped deeper into the room. Behind him came Manolo. The servant glanced nervously from side to side, his levelled Springfield rifle following the sweep of his eyes. As he reloaded the small elegant gun, Don Luis allowed his gaze to wander over the bodies of the dead *vaqueros*. Toro's body held his attention for slightly longer. He did not like what he saw. His expression showed his distaste. A movement raised his eyes to the bed across the room. On the bed Rosalia watched him apprehensively. Her hands gripped a blanket. She tugged it higher to cover her nakedness.

'Modesty is a rare virtue in a whore,' remarked Don Luis. He had finished reloading his gun. He raised it in her direction.

Rosalia shrank from the pistol pointing at her. Then she felt the coldness of the wall pressing against her bare back and she knew she could retreat no further.

'I disown you,' said Don Luis. 'Goodbye, Rosalia . . .'

'No . . . Please, no . . .' she begged. She shook her head, appealing to him with her eyes.

'You should be pleased, my dear . . .' Don Luis told her. 'Few people in Mexico are so fortunate as to die in bed . . .'

He blasted her. Rosalia's body jerked, slamming against the wall. She made a sound that reminded Don Luis of their lovemaking. Then her head sank onto the bed, staining the sheets with her blood.

Don Luis turned his attention to the wounded American. Sloane was painfully raising himself from the floor. He leaned his weight against the wall, one hand clutching the spreading red stain at his shoulder. He looked at Don Luis, his gritted teeth a mockery of a grin.

Again reloading his pistol, Don Luis strolled towards him, casually stepping over the bodies of his men.

'You have caused me much trouble, Señor Sloane,' he said. 'My first shot was aimed only to wound you. I wanted to see you suffer. My next shot will make you suffer a little more . . . And the one after will kill you.'

Don Luis pointed the Deringer, aiming low.

'Now that's what I call real ungrateful,' said Sloane. 'Shootin' me fulla holes when I been to a whole lot of trouble gettin' that skull back for you.'

He shook his head, looking pained. He didn't have to fake the pain. 'Yeah, real ungrateful . . .'

Don Luis stared at him. 'You have the skull?' he said flatly, hardly aware that he had lowered his gun.

'Uh-huh,' Sloane acknowledged, in spite of his pain enjoying the sudden change of expression in Don Luis' face.

'Where is it?' The aristocrat's voice was eager. His eyes searched the blood-splashed floor.

'Where I put it,' said Sloane. 'Where you'll never find it.'

Don Luis stiffened, his hopes of finding the skull in the room fading.

'I want that skull,' he said.

'Too bad. You should've kept that in mind 'fore you put this bullet in me.'

'Tell me where you have hidden it . . .' Don Luis spoke the words slowly and firmly, an edge of menace creeping into his voice.

Sloane looked bored.

Don Luis took a quick step towards him, raising his pistol. 'I must have that skull, Señor Sloane . . . Without it the gates of Heaven are closed to me forever!'

'I'll be sure an' wave to you from the other side,' Sloane promised.

'*Where* is it? Tell me, señor . . . If not –' Don Luis pushed the pistol in his hand meaningfully forward. Sloane eyed the Deringer with contempt. 'You kill me and you're never gonna find that skull,' he said.

Don Luis looked exasperated. He swung away from the American, unsure of his next move. Then his gaze fell on the coiled *reata* hanging from a nail. He snatched the rawhide rope off the wall and thrust it at Manolo.

'Tie him,' he instructed his servant. To Sloane he said, 'If you give Manolo any trouble – I shall be regrettably forced to kill you.'

'Looks like you got me right where you want me,' said Sloane. He let Manolo push him into a chair and tie his arms behind his back whilst Don Luis kept him covered.

'Good,' said Don Luis when Sloane was sitting helpless before him. 'Now you will please tell me where is the skull . . .

'Funny, I can't seem to remember,' said Sloane after considering the question.

Don Luis controlled his anger with difficulty. 'Perhaps this will remind you,' he said. He slapped Sloane across the face a few times. When he'd finished he blew on his heated hand.

'Now maybe you remember?'

Sloane shook his head. 'Nope, it's gone clean out of my mind,' he said.

Don Luis' hand gripped Sloane's bloodied shoulder. He pressed his thumb into the raw wound and savagely twisted the skin. Sloane's whole body jerked with the agony that shot through him. He sucked on his teeth, his tight-pressed lips holding back the scream fighting to escape from inside. Don Luis withdrew his hand and wiped it clean on a lacy handkerchief.

'Please, Señor Sloane,' the aristocrat appealed, 'tell me where is the skull and spare us this unpleasantness . . . Spare yourself further pain . . .'

155

'Guess you win,' Sloane mumbled resignedly after he'd taken a few welcome gulps of air. 'Left it by that cannon of yours – all nicely wrapped up for you.'

Don Luis' face lit up. He nodded for Manolo to go and fetch the skull. The servant hurried from the room on his mission. Smiling down at Sloane, the thin aristocrat puffed himself up like a cock getting ready to crow.

'You know, of course, that once I have the skull – there is no more reason for me to permit you to live?'

'I know,' said Sloane.

Manolo was not gone for long. He returned breathless, triumphantly bearing the velvet-wrapped bundle. Don Luis snatched it eagerly from him and opened it up. When he saw what was inside he gave a cry of disgust and dropped it, stepping back quickly.

At his feet lay a severed head, its neck a ragged twist of meat. It was the head of El Muerte.

His face shocked bloodless, Don Luis rounded on Sloane.

'What does this mean?' he demanded. He had difficulty keeping his voice steady.

'It means now you know for sure I've got the skull,' Sloane coolly answered. 'And that your friend the late Mister El Muerte won't be workin' for you no more . . .'

Don Luis stiffened. 'Working for me?'

'Sure, it didn't take much brains to figure out you hired him to go raidin' across the border and kill a lot of gringos. People round here plain love a bandit who kills gringos. Then when he was a big enough hero you were gonna join up with him against Juarez and make a big deal about gettin' back California and Texas for the Republic. That's what the people want to hear. They'd really go for a man who made them kinda promises, wouldn't they? They might even make a man like that President . . .'

'Who told you this?' Don Luis demanded, dropping his eyes to the gruesome object on the floor. '*Him*?'

'No,' said Sloane. 'He didn't tell me nothin' that made any sense because nothing made any sense to him. Maybe the skull did talk to him or maybe he was just crazy – but he got to believing the part he was play-actin' for you. It got so as he thought he really was Death. And then he set out to prove it. Suddenly gringos weren't enough – he wanted to kill everyone! That's when you figured it was high-time you was rid of him.'

'Which you have done very conveniently for me, Señor Sloane,' said Don Luis. 'I am very much grateful to you. When the people hear that the great El Muerte was killed by a gringo, they will come in their thousands to avenge his honour – a whole army of them! First we will chase out that traitor Juarez. Then we will make war on the United States – and take back the land that rightfully belongs to Mexico!'

'Sounds like you're gonna have yourself a lot of fun playin' soldiers, Don Luis. But I don't plan to be around when it happens.'

'Nor do I plan for you to be around,' said Don Luis.

'You want the skull. I want my life,' said Sloane. 'Put up or back off . . .'

His smile cruel, Don Luis reached out and laid a hand on Sloane's shoulder – the one with his bullet in it.

'You speak strong words for a man who is my prisoner,' he said, his hand closing in a firm grip on Sloane's shoulder. 'I have patience. I could make you talk . . .'

'I can shut up tighter'n a clam,' Sloane promised him.

Looking into the American's cold eyes, Don Luis could believe it. He took his hand from Sloane's shoulder.

'What terms do you suggest?' he asked.

'Only that you let me ride out of here after I've given you the skull.'

'Very well, you have my word.'

'Your word as a gentleman?' Sloane asked wryly.

'Of course!'

'All right, I'll take you to where I left it . . . but first I want a cigar.'

Don Luis made an impatient gesture.

'Got a couple right here,' Sloane told him. 'In my shirt pocket.'

Don Luis motioned his servant to help the American. Manolo obligingly dug into Sloane's pocket and came up with one of Joe's stogies. It was a very battered-looking cigar.

'It'll do,' said Sloane.

Manolo lit it for him and placed the cigar between his lips. Sloane clamped it between his teeth and took a puff. He nodded his satisfaction.

'You understand, of course, that I cannot permit your arms to be untied until I hold the skull in my hands,' said Don Luis. He moved his shoulders in an impeccable gesture of regret.

Sloane blew smoke. 'You'll need shovels,' he said.

Sloane led them to the cannon that overlooked the grounds of the *hacienda*. He slumped down beside its monstrous black body, pointing.

'Over there,' he told Don Luis, 'six paces from the tip of the barrel . . . That's where I buried it.'

Manolo positioned himself against the cannon's yawning mouth, then counted out the six paces. He marked the spot in the ground with his heel. Don Luis joined him. They put aside their guns and each took a shovel in hand ready to dig.

Sloane leaned his aching body against the cannon, watching them. They didn't know it but he was nearer to the crystal skull than they were. He had rammed the skull down the muzzle of the cannon earlier.

'You're too far,' he shouted, squeezing the words out past the cigar clamped between his teeth. 'Come back a step!'

Don Luis and Manolo obliged. They were sharply etched against the glow of the dying fire behind them. Sloane contemplated the two men as a painter contemplates the subject of his picture.

'Manolo, you're just a little too far to the right,' he said critically. 'Move in some . . . That's much better!'

'And you, Don Luis, if you want to get your hands on that skull you're gonna have to move in about a foot from the left.'

Shovel in hand, Don Luis glared irritably at the American telling him what to do.

'If this is some trick, señor, I promise you a very long slow death . . . slow and painful!'

Sloane swivelled the cigar in his mouth indignantly. 'Why should I trick you?' he asked, innocence offended. 'Haven't you got me right where you want me?'

Reassured, Don Luis moved to the position indicated by Sloane. 'Here?' he asked, jabbing the earth with his shovel.

'There is just fine,' said Sloane taking a final look at the two men standing perfectly in line with the barrel of the cannon.

'Just fine,' he said and dipped his head low, ramming the cannon's touch-hole with the glowing tip of his cigar.

The big gun's fiery roaring belch tossed him over onto his back. He lay there on his back for some time waiting for the thunder to leave his ears, watching the smoke drift towards the stars.

Then he struggled up onto his feet. It wasn't easy because his hands were still tied behind his back. He walked over to the two broken dolls that lay twistedly smouldering on the ground. The first one he came to was Manolo. He knew it was Manolo because he recognised his shoes. Then he noticed that Don Luis was somehow still alive.

Don Luis had wanted the crystal skull of Lascara so bad. And when he had a chance to grab it – he'd let it slip through his fingers. It had slipped through the rest of him too, leaving a hole that was more like an open window than a wound.

When Don Luis saw Sloane standing over him, he feebly tried to lift his head and speak. That took a lot of guts, thought Sloane. But then Don Luis had a lot of guts. Some of them he was holding. Sloane leaned down to hear what a man who'd just been blasted by a cannon had to say. The words came in a hoarse croaking whisper but he understood them.

'Now I'll never get to Heaven,' said Don Luis.

Sloane shook his head sympathetically. 'Too bad,' he said. 'I heard it was a nice place.'

He stood there a while and watched Don Luis die. Then he turned away and headed back to the *hacienda*. He had to cut the ropes that held his hands behind his back. He had to get away before the *vaqueros* returned.

Someone was waiting for him in the darkness, someone who stepped suddenly out towards him. It was Billy Wang. In his hand he gripped Chang Fung's sword. The sword flashed towards Sloane, splitting the dark. It cut through the ropes that bound his hands. Billy thrust the sword quivering into the ground. Then he stepped back, snapping into a horse stance, ready to fight.

Sloane rubbed his chafed wrists. He looked at the young Chinaman and waited for him to speak.

'She never loved me,' said Billy. 'It was you she loved all along. I lied to you because I wanted to get her back, because I was afraid of losing her. Tonight I was gonna ride out and find her. I was gonna tell her you were dead.'

'Why didn't you?' Sloane asked tautly.

'I knew one day you'd show up. That's the kind of man you are . . . You'd come riding in out of the past – and then I'd lose her again.'

Sloane watched him, his eyes narrowed, his face a clenched fist. He had an idea he wasn't through fighting yet.

'There's only one horse out there,' said Billy. 'One horse

and two of us. Only one of us is gonna ride out of here after Su Fan ...'

'Looks like you've got a long walk ahead,' said Sloane stepping forward to move past the Chinaman.

Billy's ram-headed blow knocked him staggering back. He managed to catch his balance, swayed ...

'Remember that fight we had when we first met up?' Billy asked. 'We were evenly matched then. Now you're weak, Sloane ... You've been fighting too many people for too long. You've lost a lot of blood and now you're gonna lose some more ... You know which one of us is gonna be going' after Su Fan, don't you, Sloane? It's gonna be me!'

'I've wasted enough time listenin' to you,' said Sloane, moving forward again. He didn't get very far. The lightning kick he didn't even see slammed him to the ground.

Billy looked down at him, pity in his face. 'You should have listened to Chang Fung,' he said. 'He was right. He warned you against the Way of the Ruthless Man. But that was the path you chose. This is where it's led you and this is where it ends. Look at you, you're just about through. You're finished, Sloane ... And I'm the one's gonna finish you ...'

Sloane raised himself painfully. Maybe the Chinaman was right, he thought. It looked like he'd reached the end of the trail. His wounds were bleeding afresh and his body was racked with pain through and through. He felt very tired – more tired than he had ever felt before. He closed his eyes, summoning what Inner Strength remained. His needed time to rest. Time for his wounds to heel ...

'You gonna die down there in the dirt, Sloane – or standing like a man?'

Sloane had no time left. But he had knowledge. Knowledge Billy Wang did not share. He opened his eyes and saw Billy moving purposefully towards him. There was no pity in the young Chinaman's face now. No pity, no mercy. Only a cold determination to kill.

161

Sloane climbed to his feet. 'You remember that kick Chang Fung was gonna teach you?' he asked.

'I remember,' said Billy, closing for the kill. 'The Grand Ultimate Kick ... Tears a man's head right off his shoulders, they say ...'

'That's the one,' said Sloane. 'Watch real careful now, Billy, this may be your last ever chance to see how it's done ...'

Sloane's right foot leapt up in a high flashing arc as Billy hurled himself forward ...

Dred Jefferson chuckled richly as he loaded his wagon with dead things. The bone-picking business sure had picked up good since Sloane showed, he thought. So good he'd been seriously considering taking Sloane on as a partner. But then he'd heard how Sloane was seen riding away, heading north and looking like a man who needs to get places in a hurry.

Sloane had gone but not without keeping his promise. He'd promised Dred a head and he'd been as good as his word. Better. Over by the big cannon, beside the pyramid of sleek black cannon-balls, the bone-devil had found another smaller pyramid – of human heads all neatly stacked and waiting for him.

Naturally, Don Luis was top of the pile. He'd always wanted to be head man and he'd finally made the grade. Beneath him, Dred recognised some other old familiar faces – Toro and Aguilar and El Muerte himself. And the young Chinaman whose name he'd forgotten. Dred wondered what a Chinaman's skull was selling for at current market prices.

When he'd finished loading the wagon, Dred took a quick look around in case he'd missed any small items worth having. His face lit up when he caught sight of a flash of white amongst the green of a bush. He plunged his hand down into the bush and scrabbled around until he got a grip on the

162

object. The shape of it brought a grin to his face. It was a skull.

Triumphantly, he hauled out his prize and examined it. Then disappointment drooped his face. It was a skull all right but not a good honest bone skull. It was made of some kind of shiny glass. The jaw-bone was gone and the dome of the forehead badly chipped. Worse, the skull had no soul to it.

Dred glared at the counterfeit skull. He knew he'd never get two bucks fifty for no imitation. He felt cheated. What good was a skull to a bone-devil if it wasn't made of bone, he wanted to know. What good was it to anybody? He shook his head in disdain. Then, turning back to the wagon he flipped the skull scornfully over his shoulder.

And never looked back.

HUFFAKER
RIO CONCHOS

MASSACRE

Riot raised his right foot and kicked the door in. She was standing in the far corner of the room, her eyes glazed. The pistol she held was pointed at her own chest. 'It's all right', he whispered, 'the Comanchos have gone'.
Her expressionless eyes moved towards him and her pistol wavered, turned around and pointed straight at Riot.

When they saw the results of the Apache massacre, they set out to stalk the killers — two of them by choice, and two by force. Four men against the Apache nation, on a mission that could drench the whole southwest in flames.

Also available in the
Huffaker Western series:
FLAMING STAR
BADGE FOR A GUNFIGHTER
WAR WAGON

HUFFAKER

FLAMING STAR

HALF BREED

The blood of two nations ran in his veins. Pacer was a halfbreed, feared by the whites, despised by the redskins. And hated by both.

When the lone warrior rode down into the valley at sundown, Pacer knew that he had to choose. For Buffalo Horn carried a short war lance, and the war lance carried seven scalps on it.

Buffalo Horn was a hunter.

Also available in the
Huffaker Western series:
BADGE FOR A GUNFIGHTER
RIO CONCHOS
WAR WAGON

HUFFAKER

WAR WAGON

GUNSLINGER

He pulled the trigger as Boicourt's revolver came free of leather. Boicourt was thrown back against the bar by the wallop of the heavy slug. He stared with astonishment at Taw for a choking moment, then slipped off the side.

The bartender hopped over the bar and crouched down beside him. 'Dead', he said quietly.

JACK TAWLIN was a living legend in a land where gunmen died young. A man marked for violence.

A man who dared a hold up nobody else had the guts to try . . .

Also available in the
Huffaker Western series:
FLAMING STAR
BADGE FOR A GUNFIGHTER
RIO CONCHOS

HUFFAKER

BADGE FOR A GUNFIGHTER

GAMBLING MAN

'I know a lot about you, Cash,' Whitey said. 'How you killed a man down in San Antonio and went on the prod. You've killed three men since'.

'Five', Cash said. 'Couple didn't get written up in the papers.'

'I like a man who hates people', Whitey said. That's a man you can count on. I'm making you sheriff of Yellowrock.'

For Cash shooting a man was just a matter of figuring the odds that he'd win and collecting the money he was paid for the killing. Now the sheriff's badge said he was the law. That made the odds in his favour a whole lot sweeter . . .